David thought of callir_____
magical place, perhap_____
matter where she might be, even if she were miles
away, thousands of miles away. They would be
connected by their love for each other; she would
hear him, and they would be reunited, however
briefly.

Why had she been murdered?

Had she found peace and happiness at last?

Who was her murderer?

He opened his mouth to call her. He stayed silent.

This place wasn't magical at all, was it? He had
expected that it would be a land of dreams. But it
wasn't.

It wasn't *heaven*.

Heaven was the place he had constructed in his own
fantasies, the place that legend had built up for him
over the years he had been alive on earth.

This wasn't heaven.

This was . . .

Something in between.

Also by T.M. Wright in Gollancz Horror

T.M. WRIGHT

BOUNDARIES

GOLLANCZ HORROR

Gollancz Horror is an imprint of Victor Gollancz Ltd
14 Henrietta Street, London WC2E 8QJ

First published in Great Britain 1992
by Victor Gollancz Ltd

First Gollancz Horror edition 1992

A catalogue record for this book
is available from the British Library

ISBN 0 575 05027 6

Printed and bound in Great Britain by
Cox & Wyman Ltd, Reading

POSSIBILITIES

When I think of The Other Side I think of being reunited with loved ones who have passed over. And of being with them for eternity.

I think of eternity. No beginning. No end. It's a concept that's impossible to grasp but fun to think about.

I think that happiness will be continuous because The Other Side is the ultimate reward, after all.

And I think about love. I think that, in heaven, on The Other Side, love will be sweet and everlasting. And I think that I will have to get used to love without sex, because sex is earthbound and temporal. Because the spirit, I think—desperately rationalizing—cannot have any physical needs. It cannot need to eat, or defecate, or drink, or have sex because it no longer possesses a stomach, a colon, a tongue, genitalia. Its needs are . . . spiritual. Intellectual. Divine.

It spends eternity contemplating eternity (a pastime which may not seem very worthwhile to the earthbound, but which is probably the truest and happiest expression of the spirit).

And when I think of The Other Side, I think, too, that all these ideas may be no more valid than the babblings of Neanderthals who look at the moon and believe that it is a hole in the sky.

I think that The Other Side may be something completely unguessable.

—T.M. Wright
June 4, 1990
Ithaca, New York

BOOK ONE
A TOE IN THE WATER

ONE

These snapshots were nothing more than animal protein and a couple layers of colored dye and silver nitrate that the light got at for a microsecond. They were no more substantial than that—they weren't Anne or even representations of Anne because the animal proteins, the dyes and silver nitrate had no intention of creating representations of her.

These snapshots were a fraud because they coaxed from him only microseconds of Anne's life as he had witnessed it and remembered it. And her life could not be measured in microseconds.

So, if the police photographs, the photographs taken at her autopsy (and it was not *her* autopsy at all, was it?) showed a face as placid and blank as air, they showed only a couple hours of the existence of flesh over bone. Then the decay started in earnest and those images, as well, became a lie.

Still, he had to take these snapshots out and look

at them. There were memories of Anne that existed *around* them. They were not his only memories of her, but they were among his best memories because snapshots are often taken during the best of times.

He turned some of the snapshots over—the ones that were most appealing or called up especially memorable moments—and checked for a date or a notation, or both. Then he turned the snapshot around, looked at it again for a second, set it aside and got another from the pile. He wept as he looked at them. He didn't want to weep. He thought that if someone came to the door that he would answer it red-faced and then would have to bear up under his visitor's embarrassment. It was a kind of agony he wanted to spare himself, an agony he wanted to spare the people who came to visit him.

He got his pipe out of his sportscoat pocket and lit it from a pack of book matches on his desk. The blue tobacco smoke—it smelled of cherries— did a slow dance around his head and made his eyes sting. He put the pipe out, set it in a glass ashtray on his desk, and put the snapshots in a bottom drawer of the desk. Then he stood and went to a window at the back of the room. The window overlooked fields and hedgerows that were dark green and moist this day after a rain— *Idyllic*, he thought—and, as if the fields and hedgerows could answer, he asked aloud, "Where is Anne? Where is my sister, Anne?"

His friend, Christian Grieg—a stocky, square-faced man with gentle and expressive soft blue eyes—was at that moment sitting in a little restaurant called *Oliver*'s with a woman named Karen Duffy. He had had a close, platonic relationship with her for several years. He said, "David's on the ragged edge."

Karen said, "And for good reason."

A waiter came over and asked if everything was okay. Karen nodded—she was a tall, lithe redhead in her late thirties, quick to smile and quick to frown—and Christian said, "Sure, everything's good." The waiter went away.

Karen added, "I'd be at the edge, too." She paused, then went on, "I'd be *over* the edge, I think." She gave him a soft, quivering smile, as if in embarrassment, reached and took the last whole wheat roll from a green breadbasket at the center of the table. She said, holding it up, "You want this?"

Christian shook his head.

Karen split the roll in two with her hands and buttered one of the halves. She liked to eat. Christian thought that she ate more than he did.

He said, "I think David is suicidal."

Karen pursed her lips and set her buttered roll on her plate. "I think," she said, "that David is very depressed." She cocked her head. "You think he's weak, don't you? You've always seen him that way."

"It's not a matter of weakness, Karen. For heaven's sake, it's not a matter of weakness. The kind of loss he's had has driven other people . . ." He threw a hand into the air in frustration. He finished, "To the edge."

Karen thought a moment, then declared, "Anne was his *twin sister*. She wasn't his lover. She wasn't his wife. She wasn't his daughter. She was his *twin sister*!"

"Dammit," Christian burst out, "what's the difference, really? Sister, daughter, wife. It doesn't really matter. What matters is that they were close. Very close." He could feel a fit of temper coming on and shook his head quickly to push it away. He went on, "I'm sorry, Karen. You didn't know him. You didn't know their relationship the way I did. They were friends, just like we are. Surely you can understand that kind of relationship. If you . . . if something happened to *you*, I'd probably be feeling the same way David's feeling."

"That's a nifty way of advancing your own argument, Christian."

He looked confusedly at her. "I don't understand."

She sighed. "You're right, though. I wasn't as close to their relationship as you were. I didn't understand it the way you apparently understand it." She picked up her roll, studied it a moment, frowned, put it back on the plate. "Can we get out of here, Christian? I'm feeling hemmed in."

"Hemmed in?" he asked. "By what?"

She answered unself-consciously. "By this conversation. Let's go somewhere else."

Christian said, "Yes. Okay." He paused. "Let's go and see David."

She looked at him a moment, thought of protesting, then, with a feigned smile, nodded her assent.

Anne Case was murdered on May 9th. May 11th would have been her thirty-fifth birthday. When she awoke at 7:30—her usual waking time—on the day of her murder, she had her day planned. She was going to have a breakfast of orange juice and a rye bagel and was going to follow that with an hour's worth of work in her vegetable garden, near the south side of the house. She was growing carrots, peas, turnips, and corn. She had been pessimistic about the corn because of bad luck with it in previous years; she blamed that bad luck on various garden pests. When she was finished in the garden, she was going to go to her study and write. She wrote poetry. It was confessional, romantic, and eminently unpublishable, but she wrote it every day, and for the same reasons, she supposed, that other people wrote journals: to keep the daily events of her life and her outlooks on life in some perspective. After that—and she usually spent a half hour or forty-five minutes at it—she was going to call her brother, David Case, to confirm that he would be coming over for lunch. Anne left her house only rarely. She was an agoraphobic. It was a nearly life-long condition and she had stopped trying to fight it years before. Her house was her world, and that was okay. It was a very large house—one she had inherited upon the death of her mother and father, along with a substantial trust fund set aside in recognition of the fact that she could not work outside the home—and it served nicely as a universe all its own. There was a music room, a library, a sewing room, a sitting room, several bedrooms furnished in various styles, three full bathrooms, a parlor, a game room—in which she had installed a pool table, some pinball machines, and a video game called SPACE INVADERS—a cavernous kitchen and, on the third floor, what she referred to as a "ballroom." The floors there had been polished to a magnificent shine, three chandeliers put up, and a small stage built at one end. It was her habit, at least once a day, to drift into and quickly out of the ballroom, each of the bedrooms, the living room, the parlor. She enjoyed these rooms for mere moments at a time, peopled them with characters from her fantasies, and then went on to other things.

She often thought that she was eccentric, as well as agoraphobic. She had even thought, more than once, that she was insane. It was an idea that she discounted because she knew precisely why she did what she did in her big house. She did it because her house was, after all, her world. She did it because the presence of real people made her nervous, because the world outside her house made her breathless and light-headed.

"I was looking at snapshots," David Case explained, then glanced behind him at Karen Duffy and Christian Grieg as he led them to his study. "Snapshots," he repeated, and gave them a quivering smile.

"Snapshots," said Karen.

"Pictures of Anne?" Christian Grieg asked, although he knew the answer.

David turned his head, nodded a little, then they were at his study. He motioned with his hand toward two brown leather chairs. Karen and Christian sat in them. David sat behind his desk. "I didn't want any visitors today," he said. "But I'm glad you're here."

Karen said, "Christian was worried about you."

David smiled at that, as if pleased. He said, "I'm okay. I wasn't. Before. But I am now." He lifted his pipe from the clear glass ashtray on his desk, fingered it for a moment and set it back in the ashtray. "I know where Anne is," he said.

Christian Grieg squirmed in his chair. He knew that he was squirming and he knew that David could see him squirm, but it was all right.

David chuckled. "You're going to enjoy this, Christian," he said. "No need to be uncomfortable."

Karen Duffy felt suddenly ill at ease. She'd known David for several years, as long as she'd known Christian, and she had grown to like him immensely. There had been a period of a month or so, early on, when she had thought that he was simply another handsome, middle-aged man who was glib and whose tastes were impeccable but who had, ultimately, all the depth and character of a TV game show host. She had changed that opinion over time. She had found him to be a very private person, yes, but also very caring, a person whose passions and emotions ran very deep and fast, but who often chose to keep tight-lipped about himself and his feelings rather than burden other people. She saw this as strength, and now, looking at him, she sensed that he was going to let that strength ebb a little, that he was going to reveal his humanness, his passion. She wasn't sure how she would react.

David looked at her now and said, "Have you heard of 'the other side,' Karen?"

She answered at once, nodding nervously, "Yes, I have."

And Christian sighed, "Oh, David, for heaven's sake . . ."

"Don't!" David cut in. "Please don't, Christian. Your skepticism is not welcome or appreciated."

Christian nodded sullenly. "I'm sorry."

David said, "That's where Anne is." He paused. "She's on the other side."

In his mind's eye, Brian Fisher saw himself putting the telephone receiver back on the hook, getting up, leaving the apartment, going somewhere. Anywhere. He saw himself forgetting what had happened, after a long while, or, failing that, putting enough time and distance between himself and what had happened that it would be nothing more than a blur, an old movie out of focus. A decade would probably accomplish that, he thought. Two decades would surely accomplish it.

Then, though there had apparently been no

ringing on the other end of the line, a male voice said, "Batavia Police Department, complaint desk," and Brian said at once—as if he were courtesy-bound to respond—"Hello, yes. My name is Brian Fisher." He could say no more.

"Go on," coaxed the male voice.

Brian said nothing.

"Could you state your name again, please," said the male voice.

Brian repeated his name but could say no more.

"Is this an emergency, Mr. Fisher?"

"I don't think so," Brian said.

"Then what is the nature of your complaint, sir?"

"I had a friend," Brian answered. "Her name was Anne." He paused, let the words pile up, then let them come spilling out. "Her name was Anne, she's dead now, she was murdered, and I caused it." He waited. There was a moment's silence. Then the male voice said, with more of a sense of urgency now, "That was Fisher, *F-I-S-*"

Brian hung up.

TWO

"**N**obody's questioning the reality of your experience," said Christian Grieg.

David Case nodded from behind his desk. "That's big of you, Christian." He tried a grin, found it uncomfortable. "How *can* you question it? You were *there*, for God's sake!"

Christian leaned forward in the brown leather chair and clasped his hands. He said slowly, as if reminding David of something David had forgotten, "I wasn't *there*, I was in the boat, sure. And I was in the hospital; I was in your room. But I wasn't *there*, on the other side, with you."

Karen Duffy, trying hard not to sound peeved, said, "Please tell me what you're talking about."

Christian glanced at her, then nodded at David and explained, "David had an . . . out-of-body experience—"

David interrupted. "That's not technically correct. You're talking about astral projection when you use that phrase and that's not what happened to me. What happened to me, technically . . ." He sighed. "The experience I had was a death experience." Another uncomfortable grin appeared and quickly faded. He shook his head and looked at Karen. "I died. My heart stopped. I died." He paused. "And I went over to what is commonly called 'the other side.' "

Karen said nothing. She was confused. She looked from David to Christian and then back to David, who continued, "It was a boating accident. Christian and I and some friends were out on Oneida Lake. I fell overboard. I was drunk—I was getting drunk," he corrected, "and I went under. It was fifteen minutes before they fished me out—Christian and the others. That's a long time." He was clearly having difficulty telling the story. He looked away often—at his desk, at the window. "That's a long time." he repeated, as if to himself. "And while I was under . . ." He paused. When he continued, his mood and tone were more thoughtful. "It began then, while I was under. Classic stuff, really." He got his pipe from the glass ashtray on his desk, lost hold of it; it fell to the desktop and spilled a pinch of blackened tobacco. He stared at the spilled tobacco a moment, swept it into his hand and dumped it into the ashtray. "Classic stuff," he repeated. "And I'm sure you've heard it all before, Karen."

A hard thumping noise came from the window. The three people in the room looked over. The window was clear. David explained, "It's birds. They fly into the window. I don't know why." He got up, went to the window, looked down through it, glanced back. Christian and Karen still were seated. They were looking expectantly at him. "It's a finch," he said and went back and sat at his desk.

"A finch?" Karen asked. "You mean it's dead?"

Before David could answer, Christian said, "You could put up a bird silhouette, a hawk silhouette. That would keep them away from the window."

"I'll do that," David said. He glanced at the window. "Anne told me the same thing. She had the same problem. She said a dozen birds flew into her window—the one in her kitchen; it's a small window, in her kitchen, over the sink—and the birds flew into it when she was washing dishes. So she put up a silhouette. Yes, I think it was the silhouette of a hawk. A sparrow hawk." He stopped. He shook his head miserably. "Dammit, I miss her. Why would someone *do* that to her, Christian? I don't know why anyone would *do* that to her! I've tried to figure it out and I can't figure it out! You knew her, you both knew her, you knew her problem, and now there she is—she's still at the morgue, she's still at the damned morgue, and she has no home."

"I was protecting her," said Brian Fisher. It was a phrase he'd been practicing ever since his phone call to the police. He wanted to sound as true and as honest as he thought he was.

"Could we come in, please?" said one of the two detectives at his door. That detective was a middle-aged, balding, overweight man named Fred Collins; his eyes were dark brown, very large, and they bore an almost ludicrous sensitivity, considering his job. He spoke in a tone that was businesslike and reassuring at the same time, but it was clear from his unyielding presence and bearing that he was used to being obeyed. It was just what Brian Fisher thought he needed at that moment—someone to take over, someone to accept and acknowledge his sin and punish him for it so he could get on with the plans he had for himself.

The other detective said, "You called the station, Mr. Fisher?" That detective was shorter and thinner than Fred Collins, and his bearing was not as strong. He wore a dark blue suit, white shirt, and green tie, and he stood a foot behind Fred Collins. His name was Leo Kenner.

Brian Fisher said, nodding, "I called the station." He moved to one side and gestured to indicate his apartment. "I made some coffee."

Collins and Kenner stepped in. Collins said, "No. Thank you. We would like to ask you some questions." He glanced appraisingly about the small room as he spoke. It was neat and scrupulously clean; there was the tang of disinfectant in the air. There were, Collins judged, hundreds of books—most of them hardcover—in three large bookcases made of cinder blocks and lengths of whitish pressboard. Each of these bookcases was at the center of its own beige wall. A large Andrew Wyeth print in a simple frame was displayed on one wall, near a window. The print was of a fence and fields as seen from inside a farmhouse. Collins thought it was static and melancholy. A white, four-drawer kneehole desk stood to the other side of the window. Fisher's twin bed—a bright, multicolored quilt lay on it—and a small, mahogany chest of drawers were at the opposite end of the room. Lighting—dim—was provided by a brass, gooseneck floor lamp near the left side of the desk. The chair which apparently was used at the desk was beneath the window. Collins thought that Fisher had been sitting, looking out at the park.

The park, he saw, was alive now with children and their mothers. Collins could even hear them, faintly, through the closed window.

Brian gestured at the chair and said, "One of you can sit there."

"We'll stand," Collins said.

Brian nodded expressionlessly, went and sat in

the chair, looked up, hands clasped over his knees, and said, "I wanted to protect her. She needed that." His small, pale hands worked nervously together. He added, "I loved her." His squeaky, high tenor voice quivered. "And she was suffering."

Leo Kenner said, his tone brusque and efficient, "You're talking about Anne Case?"

Brian nodded vigorously. "Anne, yes."

Collins and Kenner were standing a few feet in front of Brian. Kenner was to the right of and just behind Collins. He'd shoved his bony hands into his pants pockets and had cocked his head slightly. Collins had crossed his arms at his chest. Together, they formed an impenetrable wall.

Seeing this pose, Brian said, "I'm not going to go anywhere."

Collins said, "We're only here to question you, Mr. Fisher."

"I killed her," Brian whispered, as if he were anticipating great pain but knew he'd be able to bear up under it. "I killed Anne Case. I'm confessing to that and I want to be punished."

Leo Kenner said, "Sir, how did you kill Anne Case?"

Brian's thin pale lips parted in surprise. He looked from Kenner to Collins then back to Kenner. "You know that, you know that!" he whined. "I don't have to tell you how I killed her. She's dead." His hands worked furiously together. Outside, in the little park, a mother called sharply to her child, "Get off of that, now!" Brian lowered his head and looked at his hands. He saw that they were clasping and unclasping; his long thin fingers made the skin on the backs of his hands bright red. He unclasped them, stood abruptly, and faced the window that looked out on the park. "I killed her with a knife," he said. "I stabbed her a great number of times. I don't know how many

times but it was a great number. More than fifty."
He swallowed noisily, turned only his head, said
to Collins, "That's right?"

Collins couldn't tell if it was a question or a
statement so he asked, "Do you believe that it is?"

"Yes," Brian said, and turned his head again.

The voice of the woman in the park called, "I
told you to get off that!" It was followed by an
obscenity.

Brian said, nodding, "It's summer."

"It's only spring," said Leo Kenner.

"What difference is the month?" Brian asked.

Detective Collins asked, "You said you stabbed
Anne Case fifty times, Mr. Fisher?"

Brian said, "I want to be punished. I killed Anne
and I want to be punished. I want to die and be
with her and tell her . . ." He looked pathetically
at the two detectives. He shook his head in confusion. "I want the death penalty for this."

Collins glanced questioningly at Kenner.

Kenner said, "At present, Mr. Fisher, there is no
death penalty in New York State."

Fisher looked as if he had been struck a physical blow.

Collins said to him, "I'd like you to come down
to the station with us, sir."

"I'm being arrested?"

"We'd like to question you further."

Without turning his head, Brian said, "No.
That's not good enough. I want you to arrest me."
He spoke in a low, tight monotone. "I want you to
arrest me and punish me. It's what I deserve. I
killed Anne Case. I stabbed her fifty times, a great
number of times. Her blood spilled all over me. I
loved her." He turned his head, then. "I was trying to protect her. You have to kill me." He turned
back, looked out the window again. Another ob-

scenity drifted up from the park. Brian went on, "It's summer. She liked summer."

"Could you get your jacket, sir," Collins suggested.

"It's too warm for a jacket."

"It's spring," said Leo Kenner.

Collins said, "Brian Fisher, I am arresting you for the murder of Anne Case. It is my duty to inform you—"

Brian threw himself through the closed window. He landed facedown at the edge of the park, three stories below.

THREE

On the way to St. Jerome's Hospital in Batavia, Brian Fisher said these words to no one in particular: "Somewhere to be." Then he smiled as if at something very pleasant, and added, "With Anne." He said nothing else, nor did he smile again in this life.

He lived for twenty-nine minutes after he hit the ground, long enough for those tending to him to put him on an operating table at St. Jerome's, start an IV of lactate of Ringer's solution, and hook up a heart monitor and EEG. Soon after that, the heart monitor and the EEG flat-lined, and the surgeon in charge declared that Brian Fisher was dead.

"It begins," said David Case, "at one end of what appears to be a very long tunnel. The tunnel widens; there's a light at the end of it. The tunnel widens, or it appears to—and that could simply be an illusion; you're going up into the tunnel and so it *appears* to widen as your perspective changes." He pushed himself away from the desk, stood, went around to the front of the desk and sat on it with his hands palm-down on its front edges and his feet on the floor. Karen Duffy decided that he was trying hard to look casual, but he didn't look at all casual, she thought. He looked like a man on the verge of a scream and she wanted to interrupt him, wanted to have him get them all something to drink, or tell him she had to use the bathroom, anything to get him to stop the flow of words that were so clearly causing him such agony. But she said nothing because she was fascinated by what he was saying.

He went on, his eyes on hers, "And that's important. Perspective is important. Because it appears"—he gave her a wistful smile—"to stay the same. There is up and down and sideways. There's warmth, cold. The need to blink. Hunger. There's even the occasional itch to scratch. It's really an incredible approximation of this life. And I think"—he tapped the side of his head—"that it all comes from in here. I think it's a way of comforting ourselves that we have not really left the earth behind. Sort of like the phantom arm. You've heard of that?"

"Yes," Karen said.

David nodded. "An arm gets amputated and for a couple of weeks it still hurts—even though it's not there, it still hurts. It's the same sort of thing when you're going through that tunnel, leaving the earth behind. Who wants to do that? Who wants to leave the earth behind? No one. I certainly didn't. So we devise this clever lie that says we're still whole, that we, indeed, still have the need to blink and the need to eat, and that we still can feel warmth and cold." His grip on the edge of the desk tightened. He shook his head. "It's sort of the ultimate rationalization. Our poor disembodied . . ."—he paused—"souls want so badly to stay *earthbound*. Christ, that's where our security and comfort lies."

Christian Grieg said, "You could be very wrong, David."

David shrugged. "I could be. Sure. But I don't think I am, Christian. I was *there*, remember."

"You make it sound like . . . like it's just a trip to Cleveland, David. And even if that's all it was— think about it—even if that's all it was, if it was just a damned bus trip to Cleveland; you get on the bus in . . . wherever, and you ride through the night, you arrive at the bus station the next morning, and you look out the windows of the bus. What do you see? Cleveland? No, you see the bus station."

"Don't minimize my experience, Christian." David's voice trembled on the verge of anger, surprising Karen.

But Christian was not going to be deterred. "You see the damned *bus station*, David. You see a parking area and a bunch of smelly buses and you see people coming and going. Then the bus that *you're still on* goes back to wherever it came from and you proclaim to the world that you have seen Cleveland and are now an expert on it."

"I went over to the other side!" David's words were clipped, harsh, angry. "I saw what was there. I experienced it. And I came back!" He closed his eyes, clearly surprised at his outburst. He sighed.

Christian said, "And you want to go there again, don't you?"

David shook his head slowly. "I know that Anne is there. And I know that I love her and I miss her—" He stopped, lifted his head. His jaw quivered. He was about to weep. "But I don't know anything," he stammered, and shook his head again. "All I really know . . . dammit, all I really know is that she's at the morgue, she's on a slab . . . she's in the *cooler* at the morgue and I don't know anything other than that." He closed his eyes. He whimpered, "My God, I wish I knew more. I wish to heaven that I knew more and that I could find her."

Detective Kenner said to Fred Collins, "I think he did it. I think he was telling us the truth."

Collins was skeptical. "So he came close on the number of stab wounds. He guessed." Collins had been typing his report on Brian Fisher's suicide. He stopped and looked questioningly at Kenner. "Leo, this ribbon's no good. You want to change it for me?"

Kenner sighed, got up, went around his desk and lifted the cover on Collins' ancient Remington Rand. "You've got the mechanical sense of a banana, Fred."

Collins shrugged. "I know."

"Uh-huh. Well, why don't you watch me do it this time, so next time you can do it yourself."

"Sure," Collins said, but his mind was elsewhere. "Like I said, Fisher guessed. He *guessed*. I mean, he could read, like everyone else." Collins was referring to the fact that the *Batavia Daily Sun* had used the phrase "multiple stab wounds" to describe the cause of Anne Case's death. "So he guessed. And he wasn't right on the mark, was he? I mean, he said he stabbed her fifty times and she was really stabbed sixty-three times, right?"

Kenner shook his head. "That doesn't mean anything, Fred. You don't really believe that a killer is going to stop and *count* the number of times he stabs someone, do you? Of course he isn't. He's acting under a compulsion. He's in a frenzy. I remember a case from a couple of years ago—some kid high on PCP stabbed his little brother thirty times, but when we asked the kid about it, he said, 'Yeah, I stabbed him three times.' And the kid *believed* it, Fred. Hell, if you stab someone *once*, that's memorable; you stab him again, it's a little less memorable. And if you go on from there, over and over again, it becomes a blur, like trying to count the number of thrusts you make during an orgasm. It's the same thing. It's compulsion. It's frenzy. Hell, you're out of your head, you don't know what you're doing." He took the ribbon from Fred's typewriter. He shrugged. "Maybe you know what you're doing, Fred. Sure you do. But there's no way you can stop yourself from doing it."

Collins said, "That's still a long way from proving that Fisher was guilty."

Kenner opened the top right-hand drawer of Collins' desk, got a new ribbon from it, and tossed the old one into the metal wastebasket near his desk. "His confession means something, Fred. It really does." He stooped over and began putting the new ribbon in Collins' typewriter. "Now watch me here, okay? I don't want to have to do this for you again."

Two hours later, David got a phone call from Detective Collins. Christian Grieg and Karen Duffy had left an hour earlier and David was preparing a light supper.

Detective Collins said, "Mr. Case, I have something to tell you."

"Yes?"

"Today a man named Brian Fisher committed suicide."

"My God," David breathed.

"Did you know him?"

"Yes."

"Was he your sister's lover?"

"I can't ... Yes." He paused. "He was her lover."

"Mr. Case, Brian Fisher confessed to me that he murdered your sister."

David said nothing.

Detective Collins coaxed, "Did you hear what I said to you, Mr. Case?"

Still, David said nothing.

"Are you all right, sir?"

David whispered, "He murdered her?" His voice was low and harsh.

"I'm sorry," said Detective Collins. "I didn't understand what you said."

David said, "Brian Fisher told you that he murdered Anne?" His tone was tight with anger.

"Sir, I would like to speak with you in person about this. Could you come here, to the station? Do you know where it is?"

"Dammit," David shouted, "answer my question. Did you say that Brian Fisher *murdered* my sister?"

"What I said, Mr. Case, was that he confessed to your sister's murder. You should know, however, that a confession in and of itself—"

"Where is he now?"

"As I told you, he took his own life. This afternoon. At his house near Austin Park."

"I *know* that he committed suicide, Detective. That's not what I asked. I asked where he is."

Detective Collins said after a moment, "Perhaps I'd better come over there, Mr. Case."

"Please answer my question," David insisted.

"Sir, Mr. Fisher's body is at the county medical examiner's office—"

"And *that* isn't what I asked, either. I want to

know where *he* is. Not where his body is. It's very simple. Where is Brian Fisher?"

"Sir, could you please stay there. I'm going to come over."

David said, "Because I'll tell you where he is, Detective. He's free. He's escaped responsibility for his crime. He thinks he's gotten off to where no one can touch him."

"Mr. Case—"

"But he's wrong, Detective. He's very wrong."

FOUR

In the room, there were big, sturdy wooden chairs, and wide, overstuffed couches that nobody ever sat in; there was an empty bookcase, and a floor lamp minus a cord and switch. There were paintings on the wall, too—each a simple wedding of color and line, like an Easter parade seen through dust.

The room opened onto half a dozen other rooms similarly furnished. There were no doors between the rooms, and no doors at all in the house, not even in the entranceway, or in the back, where the kitchen led out to a thousand acres of clover. There were openings for doors, but no doors.

There were openings for windows, but no glass.

The house was like many others. It was the way houses were built here, as if planned from a memory that was incomplete.

People came and went from these houses, but

no one claimed ownership of them and no one spent any time in them.

That was the way things were here, too.

The house was made of pine and green clapboard put together with common nails. It had two stories and an attic, a front porch, a back porch, and a cellar.

The creatures that existed in the cellar might, upon a quick glance, have been mistaken for creatures that lived in many cellars. They burrowed into wood and dug holes in the ground. They made noises at night. And if the light was right, their eyes shone. They were creatures of the darkness, and they were as old as humankind. People had created them and people sustained them.

On occasion, rain came to the area where the house had been built. It pelted the stone tile roof, cascaded over the edge to the ground, soaked in, and was gone. Evaporation did not exist here.

Sometimes, people danced in the house and around it.

The people had no names. In this place, no one did.

David filled up his five-year-old Subaru at a Chevron station on Route 96, a couple of miles east of Batavia, and then picked up a hitchhiker who rode with him for a half hour. David often picked up hitchhikers. After college, in the late sixties, he had spent several months hitchhiking across the United States and Canada—"an oddysey of self discovery," he had called it—and he knew what it felt like to wait for hours for a car to stop. The hitchhiker tried to strike up a conversation, but David explained that he was not in the mood for talk, so the hitchhiker fell quiet until David dropped him off just outside Rochester, when he said, "Thanks, enjoy your trip."

David was driving to Syracuse, New York, 120 miles east of Batavia. He owned a cabin on Oneida Lake. It had been in his family for half a century and it was just barely habitable. It had flooded regularly, had been repaired regularly, and David had recently made plans to have it bulldozed and a new building erected.

He sang along with whatever was on the radio as he drove. It was a habit, and he was seldom aware of it, especially now, with his mind on other things—on his sister, on Brian Fisher, on questions of life and death, rebirth and retribution.

David had a small, black steel case in the car with him. It was about the size of a cash box, and it had a three-position combination lock built into it. The case contained several doses of A2d-40, a drug in testing at Laude Pharmaceuticals in Batavia, where David had worked for ten years as a pharmacological researcher. A2d-40 was designed to lower body temperature and metabolism during surgery, and inhibit blood flow. It had been in testing and development at Laude Pharmaceuticals for five years and there were problems with it. Its side effects were minimal—possible memory loss, possible clotting factor difficulties in older patients—but the tolerance level of individual patients to the drug varied widely. A few cc's might produce the desired effects of lowered body temperature and metabolism in some patients, while other patients might experience coma. These results had been demonstrated only in animal testing. The drug had yet to be tested on a human being.

In the room, a man wept. His weeping was soft and unself-conscious. While he wept he also smiled. Eventually, his smile changed to laughter and his weeping grew more intense, so he was laughing and crying at the same time.

The man was new to this place. He had come into the house, and into the room, because it was familiar, as were weeping and laughter, and he desperately needed the familiar.

Ninety miles east of Batavia, David stopped at a roadside restaurant to have coffee. He spent a quarter of an hour chatting with the waitress because he was her only customer and she seemed to need to chat. Then he got back into his Subaru and continued driving. He realized before long that he was hungry. It was not an overwhelming hunger, not something he couldn't ignore. So he did ignore it.

The house was empty.
Darkness came.
The creatures that lived in the cellar moved gracefully, like water, up the stairs and across the floors, through the doorways and over the windowsills, out into the fields of clover.
Nothing moved in these fields. So the creatures returned to the cellar.
Light came.

Twenty miles west of Oneida Lake, the Subaru backfired, coughed, and its engine shut down. David pulled the car to the shoulder, got out and opened the hood. He was miserably incompetent with engines—he could, he realized, have just as easily been looking into the guts of a refrigerator. He took the air cleaner off, peered into the carburetor, watched tendrils of light gray smoke rise out of it. This was okay, he decided; carburetors were where the gasoline and air mixture ignited, so of course there was smoke. He put the air cleaner back, checked the oil. The crankcase was full.

He told himself that he was in no hurry. But that, he knew, was a lie. He closed the hood, got back into the car, tried to start the engine. It turned over, backfired, then died. He waited a few moments, then tried it again. This time the car started and he pulled onto the road and continued his trip.

He thought, not for the first time, that he had not been able to say good-bye to Anne. It was the kind of mistake that God made from time to time—fashioning a death without the chance for good-byes. It was cruel and unfair, and for most people there was no chance to rectify it.

There had been no explanations, either. No answers. Only an aching point of emptiness. One moment she was alive. And then she was dead. As if she had rounded a hill in a car and had collided head-on with a truck. No time for explanations. No time for answers. Merely an instant of violence, followed by a lifetime of separation.

It was warm in the car. He reached over and covered the black steel case on the seat next to him with his white jacket. The drug inside the case was susceptible to light and to temperature extremes. It also kept poorly. At Laude Pharmaceuticals, it had a shelf life of three days.

David passed over a long bridge and turned on the radio; a Beatles tune came on. He listened to it a few moments, switched channels, got a Simon and Garfunkel song, and turned the radio off.

He found that he was weeping softly and he realized that he had been weeping for some time as thoughts of Anne had come to him. Weeping for her pain, for the abrupt change in her existence, for the end of a routine she had grown comfortable with—like the trauma a fetus experiences when it is thrust out of the soft and warm world of the womb and into a world of cold, and of hard edges.

Death, he thought, *is the end of our comfortable routines*.

He slowed the car and made a sharp right onto Route 12. Oneida Lake was fifteen miles west. He'd be at the cabin within twenty minutes.

It was daylight in the room and nothing moved, except the dust. It covered everything. It moved as if from the force of wind, though there was no wind. It rose and scattered and collected itself, it wafted into the space of the room, settled, and collected.

The dust was dark. Like the earth.

It was made of earth.

FIVE

THE FOLLOWING DAY

Christian Grieg angrily put the phone down and looked at Karen Duffy, seated on a white loveseat nearby. He snapped, "David took some damned drug. He's in a hospital in Syracuse."

Karen looked at him a moment, then asked, incredulous, "Suicide?"

Christian answered, "I don't know." He paused. "He admitted himself to the hospital, but it sure sounds like suicide, doesn't it? It sure as hell *sounds* like it!" He crossed the room to the closet, got his coat. Karen stood. He said to her, "You're coming with me, right?"

"To Syracuse?"

"Yes."

She nodded. "I'd like to."

He gestured at her short brown coat on the back of the loveseat. "Good. Then get your coat, and we'll leave."

* * *

In the five days since Anne's death, a patina of dust had collected in her big house.

A window in a first floor room had been left open and two martins had come in through it. They had flown happily about in the cavernous first floor, then had flown up to the second floor. Now, they couldn't find their way back to the open window. But they weren't hungry. Small insects had flown in through the same window.

Spiders lived in the house, too, especially in the third floor ballroom, whose door was open. Eventually, the martins would find their way to the ballroom.

At the kitchen sink, water dripped. It was a small and slow drip. It hit the side of the drain, slid over the edge and went down almost soundlessly.

In a second floor bedroom, a nerve plant drooped from thirst.

In the parlor, a weight-driven wall clock stopped.

Flies had begun to dehydrate on windowsills.

The doctor at Syracuse General said to Christian Grieg and Karen Duffy, "He's recovering. It looks good. The prognosis is good." The doctor was a chunky man with a round, red face and small gray eyes. He paused, then went on, "The drug he took was unknown to us, so we were uncertain how to deal with it, as you can imagine, but the prognosis is good for a quick recovery. Thank goodness he admitted himself, otherwise . . ." They were standing outside David's room. They had yet to go in. The door was partway open and Karen could see that David was awake, with his gaze on the ceiling. She said, "Then he really did try to kill himself?"

The doctor nodded at once. "It bears all the ear-marks of a suicide attempt, yes. He told us he had made a mistake. That was the word he used. 'Mistake.' He denies that he was attempting suicide. He denies it quite vehemently, in fact."

"Of course he does," Christian whispered; then, louder, "May we see him now?"

"For a few minutes," the doctor answered. "He's weak, as you can imagine, so please don't tax him unduly."

"We won't," Christian said. He took hold of Karen's arm and they went into David's room.

David was remembering that there had been no light at the end of the tunnel, that there had been darkness, as if night had fallen, and a sky filled with . . . what? Not stars. Not the Big Dipper here, Orion there, Cassiopea, the Pleiades. Not stars, but patterns of energy, as if he were looking through a dark blanket at the rising sun.

And the sounds all around him had been at once familiar and unfamiliar, like a recording of night sounds played backward at slow speed.

"What?" he'd whispered. And he'd heard himself, though his voice had sounded distant, as if *he* were being whispered to.

He'd been lying on his left side with his right arm down so his hand was on his upper thigh and his left arm was up, as if he were reaching.

He had felt no pressure beneath him, no tug of gravity. He had, oddly, felt pressure from above.

Then, in an instant, he was in the tunnel again, and its mouth was receding, and he had felt as if he were falling.

And he had felt very, very afraid.

Consciousness had seemed like a reprieve.

* * *

"Look at us," he heard. It was Christian's voice; he knew that Christian was in the room, and that Karen was with him, but he did not turn to look.

"Please," said Karen.

"No," David said.

A few moments of silence followed, then Christian said, "Why did you do it?"

David said nothing.

Karen said, "Tell us why you did it, David. We need to know."

David said, his gaze still on the ceiling, "I didn't do what you believe I did. I *couldn't* do that."

Christian said at once, "You took some damned drug, right? Tell us what we're *supposed* to believe."

David said nothing. He wanted to tell them to leave; he didn't need their criticism, their pity, or even their understanding, now.

Christian repeated, "You took some damned drug," paused, then added, with emphasis, "*right?*"

David nodded a little.

"Then it's self-explanatory."

Karen admonished, "This is not the time to be judgmental—"

"The hell it isn't," Christian cut in. "This is *exactly* the time. What better time is there, Karen? This is my friend, here, and for some damned stupid reason, he—"

"I went over," David cut in. He did not turn his head to look at them. "I went over to the other side." He looked at Christian, saw that the muscles of the man's square face were rigid, as if in anger, and that his large gray eyes were wide with disbelief.

"I'm not going to listen to it," Christian managed, as if preparatory to leaving the room. But he stayed where he was.

Karen said, her voice low, clearly embarrassed, "I'm sure you *believe* that, David—"

"I don't *believe* it, I *know* it." He waited a moment for his sudden anger to subside. He looked away again, at the ceiling. "I'm sorry," he whispered. "But it's simply not a matter this time of belief or disbelief. I went over to the other side, again, and it . . . scared the hell out of me."

Christian said, "They're probably going to charge you. Attempting suicide is illegal—"

Karen admonished, "Please, Christian."

"No," David said. "Let him talk. I know this confuses him. Of course it confuses him." He looked at Christian. "Forgive me," he said.

Christian said, still angry, "It's weak, it's a weak thing you did. Weak and selfish." He paused. "And damned unnatural, too."

David gave him a quick, puzzled look. "You don't understand. I went looking for Anne. And for him, too. For Brian Fisher. I *must* find them, I *have* to find them."

"Why?" Karen asked.

David looked earnestly at her. "Karen, it's clear, isn't it? I need to know *why* she died. I have to know the reason for it. I need to know if she's happy, now." He looked away. His eyes misted over. "And I need to find *him*, too!"

"Him?" Karen asked.

"Brian Fisher. My sister's murderer. He thinks he's gotten away with something. But he hasn't. He probably thinks that he's punished himself for my sister's murder—but it's not good enough, it's not nearly good enough!"

"Goddammit!" Christian whispered.

SIX

In the room the days came and went like leaves turning over in a wind. Time was not measured well by them; the days measured only the passing of events—snow fell and covered the house to a depth of several inches, then was gone; a breeze passed through the house, pushed the dust about, and when it dissipated, the dust collected itself again.

The dust was sturdy and flesh-colored. It sat up a little as it collected itself, then it lay down again.

In the cellar, during the passage of darkness, the things that lived there slithered up the stairs, out the doors and over the windowsills, and found the fields of clover empty.

They went back to their cellar.

And they waited.

* * *

Christian Grieg said, "I've told you this before, David—I think you sound flaky when you talk about going over to the other side."

David was surprised. "You never told me that," he said. It was the morning after Christian and Karen's first visit, and he was sitting up in his hospital bed and thinking that he felt good. "You said you *believed* me," he went on.

"No, David. I never believed you. And if I haven't told you before that you sounded flaky, then I meant to."

Karen said, trying to be the peacemaker, "This is getting nowhere."

"We've nowhere at all to go," Christian snapped. "This is a dead end. We're visiting our friend who's crazy, our friend who tried to kill himself." He shook his head. "There's nothing to discuss, there's nowhere to *go*, Karen."

David said, "I've never heard you sound like this before, Christian."

Christian smiled. It was as quick as a pulse beat, and as tiny as the smile of a baby that has burped, but David saw it and wondered about it. Christian hurried on, his mouth set and serious, "I don't understand you, David. I don't think I've *ever* understood you. And it doesn't make me feel good. You're my friend, and I think I'm *supposed* to understand you. But here's the thing; if I don't understand *you*, then how can I understand anyone?"

David said, "What is there to understand? There is *this* world. And there is *another*. And, regardless of what you believe or understand, I went from *here* to *there*." He looked apologetically at Karen. "It's true, Karen. Everything I've told you and Christian is true."

"Yes," she said, "I know that, I understand that." But she was clearly at sea. She shook her head a little, gave him a small, nervous grin, looked at Christian, who was stone-faced, then back at David. "I believe that *you* believe it, David. That's important, I think."

He sighed. "Yes, well thank you for that," he said. "Now, I'm sorry, but I'm going to have to ask you both to leave. They're coming to give me some damned shot in a couple of minutes, and I'd like some privacy."

"Of course," Karen said, and got her coat from the back of a chair nearby.

Christian said, still stone-faced, his voice crisp and knowing, "You'll have to talk to us sooner or later, David. We're your friends. You can turn your back on us, but we'll still be here."

David gave him a long, studied look. He saw the man smile once more, the same kind of smile he'd seen on him a few minutes earlier, and again he wondered about it. He decided that it was not a nervous smile—the kind that one friend gives another when he doesn't know what to say, or what to think. It was the kind of smile that has guilt and satisfaction in it. And secrecy. The kind that is little more than a twitch. He said, "Yes, Christian, I'll talk to you. I'll have a lot to say, in fact."

"Good," Christian said. "It's best for everyone. Come to grips with it David. This is a heinous thing you've done. It's a crime against yourself. It's appalling and unnatural."

David said nothing. He had never before seen Christian so archly judgmental and he wasn't sure how to react to it.

"Good," Christian repeated, and a moment later he and Karen left the room.

The martins that had gotten closed up in Anne Case's empty house had found their way to the third floor ballroom and were going after the spiders that lived there. There were audacious jumping spiders, daddy longlegs, a brown recluse; and there were far more spiders than the martins could eat in a day. Most of the audacious jumping spiders—whose eyes were much better than the eyes of other spiders—had seen the martins and were busy finding hiding places.

There were many places for the spiders to hide. There was a set of tall cupboards in four of the room's six corners. These cupboards were for towels or clothes or dancing shoes, all of which were items that, at one time or another in the house's one hundred-year history, had been in use in the room. There were also built-in bookcases whose shelves did not all fit flush with the wall, and some of the spiders hid on the back edges of these shelves. A half dozen of the spiders also hid in the tall lace curtains at the bay windows, although the martins spotted two of these spiders easily and made quick work of them.

The martins called to each other as they flew about the room. Their song was high-pitched, but musical, and the martins liked the way it echoed from the walls of the huge room; in fact, the younger of the two birds was convinced for a moment that there were other birds in the room.

In the basement of the house, there was a tiny gas leak. It was not a potentially explosive leak, but on still days, when a breeze could not push through the cold air-vents and into the basement, the leak built up and smelled bad. Creatures that lived in the basement had died because of the leak. The newborns of a dormouse, which had made its nest in a corner of the basement near the leak, were now struggling mightily to stay alive while their mother rushed frantically about, with no idea what was happening. Eventually, using an instinct that was far more useful to it than naked intelligence, it would relocate the nest, and its children would survive.

On this day, two sturdily built middle-aged women in crisp gray business suits came to the front door of the house and knocked firmly. Each of the women had a bible tucked under her arm and a sheaf of *Watchtowers* in hand. When they got no answer to their knock, they knocked again. They wore pleasant, forgiving smiles which did not alter even as the women went back to their car and drove away.

The doctor attending to David introduced a man who was tall, very thin, and almost comically intense looking. "This," said David's doctor, "is Dr. Flexner. He's a psychiatrist and he would like to speak with you for a few minutes, if you're up to it."

David gave both men a noncommital smile, but said nothing.

"Are you up to it, Mr. Case?"

David said, "If he is."

Dr. Flexner nodded a little, as if to himself. He said, in a voice that had the jarring quality of being sepulchral and nasal at the same time, "I have looked at your file, Mr. Case. I find it, and you, quite interesting."

"Thank you," David said.

"Thank you? For what?"

"For finding me interesting."

"Well, of course, all people are interesting—"

"Yes, they are," David agreed.

Dr. Flexner smiled tightly, as if realizing he was being toyed with. He said, speaking slowly and succinctly, the nasal quality in his voice now very obvious, "I would like to talk with you specifically about your visits to what you refer to as 'the other side.' I have worked with other people, I can tell you, who have claimed similar . . . odysseys." He smiled again, coyly. "I myself have had such an experience, and I must say that it was quite horrifically convincing."

David said, "I think horrific is the wrong word, Doctor."

"Yes," Flexner said, " 'horrific' is entirely the wrong word. And of course there is the fact that you have recently lost a loved one to a tragic event."

David looked at Flexner for a long moment. Then he said curtly, "I'm sorry, but I'm really not up to this, now. I hope you understand."

"And you can well imagine," Flexner went on, his tone crisp, authoritarian and nasal, "that such an event could trigger impulses that might lead to self-destruction. It is a given in cases of severe depression. It is the set of your emotions which drives you; and so we must alter that set of emotions, Mr. Case."

David wasn't looking at him. He was looking at his feet sticking out from beneath the blanket. He had his arms folded. His face was expressionless. Under other circumstances, he would have been thinking that Dr. Flexner was an ass. But he was thinking, instead, about his sister, about Brian Fisher, and about answers he did not have. Flexner went on, clearly annoyed, "Sir, if this is the wrong time—"

"It is," David said. "As I've said already."

"Then there will be another time," Flexner said and, with David's attending physician following him, he left the room.

David had visited his sister often, and had sometimes spent the night in one of the many unused bedrooms on the second floor. On the nights when he stayed, he occasionally woke early in the morning because he could hear her moving about in the dark house. It had been a nearly lifelong habit with her—getting up in the wee hours to walk by herself in the darkness. "It's good for thinking, and for dreaming," she explained, "to walk in the dark, in a house that I know."

Often, she sang in a small, barely audible voice. The songs she sang would have been unrecognizable to a casual listener because she sang so softly. The songs that David heard were, he guessed, songs that their mother sang to them both when they were very young, songs that had usually accompanied them into sleep. Ironic, he thought, that Anne, as an adult, should sing them as she walked through her house late at night.

On an overnight visit six months before her murder, David woke, saw her padding past his door, and called, "Anne? Is everything all right?" He had never called to her before upon waking in the small hours to find that she was up and about, and he wondered what had made him call out to her now.

She did not answer him at once. He heard her stop walking—that is, he heard nothing. Then, moments later, she reappeared in the open doorway. A diffused yellow light shone from somewhere beyond her, and he could see little more than her soft profile. She said. "Did I wake you, David? I'm sorry." Her voice was low, concerned.

"Is everything all right?" he said again.

"Why do you ask?" It was an evasion, and he knew it. She went on, "You've seen me walking in the house late at night before."

After a moment's hesitation, he said, "What's wrong, Anne?"

And, after only a moment—because obfuscation and evasion between them were uncommon things—she answered, "I've made a mistake." She sighed. It had the odd quality of being both fearful and resigned. "I've made a very bad mistake, David."

He got out of bed—he was wearing boxer shorts and a T-shirt—crossed the room, put his hands on her shoulders. Behind her, the hallway stretched for twenty feet in both directions. David noticed again the diffused yellow light he had seen from the bed, but it was brighter here, at the door. He stuck his head out the doorway, looked right and left. He saw that all the lights were on in the large, open room to the right, and over the stairs to the left. This was odd. Usually, when Anne walked the house at night, she walked it in almost total darkness.

"You've got all the lights on," he said.

She nodded. "Yes. Downstairs, too. I didn't want to turn the light on here"—in the hallway—"because I thought it would disturb you." A brief pause. "I never knew before what was in the darkness. Do *you* know?" She paused, then continued, her voice low, as if she were sharing some awful secret, "It hides monsters, David. The darkness hides monsters."

"Anne—"

She put her fingers on his lips. "No. It's all right. I want to talk about it. Believe me I do. But not now. I have a lot of thinking to do now. Perhaps in the morning. Okay?"

"I don't understand—"

"Please, David, go back to bed. We'll talk. In the morning."

And because he was her brother, and knew her as well as anyone, he realized that any resistance would be futile. "Yes, in the morning," he said, turned, and went back to bed. When he looked toward the doorway again, she was gone. He fancied he could hear her padding about in the large open room at the end of the hallway, fancied he could hear her singing. But he knew that he couldn't. This night, he realized, was very different from other nights. This night, there were monsters in the house.

But he and Anne did not talk the following morning. She was making breakfast when he arrived in the kitchen, her mood cheerful and talkative, so he thought he had better wait until she brought up the subject of the night before. But she never did.

SEVEN

In the dark room, the dust collected itself, and stood. It looked about, and was frightened.

The dust felt no tug of gravity. It felt a tug from above. This was, at once, strange and comforting.

Eventually, the dust collected itself sufficiently that it scratched at an itch that had always bothered it. Then it stood and, without real purpose, moved about in the room. At last, it went back to where it had arisen.

It lay down.

It wept.

It laughed.

As strange as this place was, it was oddly familiar, too, and the dust desperately needed the familiar.

Detective Fred Collins was off work and he was thinking about Anne Case. Collins lived alone in a three-room apartment on a pleasant street on Batavia's east side, and when he did not have to work, he stayed in his apartment, listened to soft rock music—The Carpenters, Carly Simon, early Beatles and Beach Boys—and thought about his work, and about the people he dealt with, both the living and the dead. What he was thinking about Anne Case was that she had been doomed from the beginning of her life. He had no hard and fast reason for thinking this. He had not known her in life. He had first lain eyes on her a week earlier, when she'd been dead for half a day and her body had had sixty-three stab wounds in it, most of them concentrated in her stomach and in her upper back. When he saw her then, he thought that she had looked strangely serene, as if she had died in her sleep. It was true that many murder victims looked passive, as if they were sleeping, and that was simply because, in death, the muscles relaxed. But few of the dead actually looked serene, as Anne Case had. And that was why Fred Collins was thinking that she had been doomed from the beginning of her life, because she had clearly been living it in preparation for that moment—the moment of her death.

Fred Collins whispered to himself, "You don't know what you're talking about." He supposed that these thoughts were no more than mental games he played because he was trying to humanize the people he dealt with. It may or may not have been correct that Anne Case was doomed from the start of her life, but it didn't matter because he always kept such ideas to himself.

He had begun to believe that Brian Fisher was not her murderer. It was a doubt he had expressed once to his partner, Leo Kenner, who had guffawed and said, "Sure he was, Fred. Of course he was. He murdered her because he loved her. That's obvious."

Collins shook his head. "People don't murder the people they love, Leo."

"People murder whoever's available—*especially* the people they love."

"I know what you're saying, and I think you're wrong. He didn't . . . this Brian Fisher didn't *possess* her, he really did *love* her. I'm convinced of it. And I don't think he murdered her. I think he may have *blamed* himself for her murder, but he didn't actually do it." He paused "And there's this 'frenzy' thing you were talking about, too, which doesn't hold up."

"Frenzy thing?"

"Yes. She was stabbed sixty-three times. We know that. We counted the wounds."

"So?"

"So it doesn't add up to frenzy, Leo. It adds up to . . ." He paused. "Here I am, I'm the murderer, and I've stabbed her—what?—twenty or thirty times in the stomach, and now, just to make it look *symmetrical* . . . I don't know, just so it won't look *half-assed*, hell, I'll turn her over and stab her another twenty or thirty times in the back. That's not *frenzy*, Leo. That's premeditation."

But in the end, Collins had felt certain that he'd convinced Kenner of nothing; Kenner had, in fact, made him feel as if he were impossibly naïve and a little addlepated besides, so Collins had said nothing more about it.

Today, in his apartment, Anne Case would not leave him. He wondered about her life, about her growing up, about her passions, her last morning, her last moments alone.

He thought that she had been softly attractive. People used to use the word "frail" to describe people like her. He had heard about her agoraphobia and had thought, yes, she looked the type, the type to *prefer* wandering about in her big house all alone.

He did not think that her death was a sad thing. If this had been his first case, his second, his third, he would have been torn up by the fact of a life so quickly and cruelly taken, by the pain she had clearly suffered, and by her aloneness. But after so many years dealing with the dead, he had grown beyond that. Her murder had not been sad. Her death had not been sad. Her *life* had been sad because she had been doomed from its start to constant agony, and to a terrible death.

The afternoon following Christian and Karen's visit to his room at Syracuse General, David was visited by Detective Leo Kenner, who showed David his badge, introduced himself, and asked, "Do you remember me?"

"Yes," David said.

"May we talk?" Kenner put his shield back in his coat pocket.

"How did you know I was here?"

"From your place of work. Your doctor called them to find out what he could about this drug you took."

"Oh," David said. "Of course."

"May we talk?" Kenner repeated.

"I doubt that there's much to say," David said.

"Perhaps I could be the judge of that."

David was still in his pajamas; he gestured toward the closet. "Will you excuse me a moment while I get some clothes on?"

"I won't take much of your time," Kenner answered. He was tall and stocky, and his body presented an almost impenetrable wall between David and the closet. "I'd simply like to ask you one or two questions."

"What questions? About Anne?"

"About Brian Fisher."

"I didn't know him. I met him once. Twice. We shared a Christmas dinner at Anne's house last year; he was quiet, I would say he was shy. Painfully shy. I respected that; I let him be. We've said maybe three or four sentences to each other."

"Did your sister talk about him?"

"Anne wasn't much of a talker."

"She said nothing about him?"

"Of course she did. She said that he treated her well and that she was happy when they were together. She didn't elaborate."

"Would you say, Mr. Case, that they had a passionate relationship?"

"I have no idea what they did in *bed*, Detective—"

"I'm not talking about that, Mr. Case. I'm talking about their . . . commitment to each other. Was it strong? Would you say that they loved each other very deeply?"

David said nothing.

"Mr. Case?"

"Yes," David whispered.

Kenner said, "Yes, they were deeply in love with each other?"

David said aloud, "They loved each other as much as two people can. It was obvious to anyone. If they had walked together outside that house then people would have pointed at them and smiled and said how nice they looked, what a beautiful couple they made." He paused, looked away, again as if in reflection. He looked back, nodded. "Yes, Mr. Kenner. They loved each other." He shook his head a little. "It went beyond love, I think." He looked away again. Kenner could see that David was being swept by emotion, so he decided it was a good time to push on.

"And do you believe that Mr. Fisher murdered your sister?"

David didn't answer for a moment, then he said sharply, "Yes. Of course." He stopped. His breathing had suddenly become heavy and ragged with emotion. He looked away and continued, "I don't know." He shook his head. His eyes watered. "I don't know," he whispered. Another pause. "Yes." He was still looking away. "He could have murdered Anne. Of course he could have murdered Anne."

"Thank you, sir," Kenner said.

In the room it was daylight and the dust had gathered itself together and had become a man.

EIGHT

Karen Duffy felt ill at east, alone in Christian Grieg's house. She had no concrete reason for it. It was not an uncomfortable house; it was small, tastefully furnished, and it had that welcoming, lived-in air that so many houses lacked. She had, in fact, spent more than a few happy hours in it with Christian. But lately, when he left her alone there, it was as if he left some part of himself behind to watch her. And she had no concrete reason for feeling that way, either, because she had always thought of Christian as an open and generous man who cared little for possessions, per se, and who was clearly happy to share whatever he had with his friends. Still, she felt ill at ease. And today, while he was gone, she stayed in the living room and read a book while she waited for him to return.

After a while, she decided that she did not know Christian as well as she thought she had, and that was the reason for her discomfort. She imagined that there was some facet of himself that he kept hidden, that possibly it was something dark. But, soon, she decided that she was merely trying to find a reason for her discomfort, and that giving Christian a "dark side" was as good a reason as any.

She wondered suddenly if his personality had altered in the last couple of months? It was hard to say; she didn't know. He did not seem to have a tight rein on his temper anymore. Ever since she'd known him, he had seemed to be a man who kept his anger in check. There was the time, for instance, when a man who had been tailgating Christian had run into him at a stop sign. Christian had merely shaken his head resignedly, gotten out, and politely exchanged all the necessary information with the man. Karen wasn't sure what the Christian she knew now would do under the same circumstances.

His treatment of David was odd, too. So judgmental, so lacking in understanding and good will. He and David had been friends for many years, and the old Christian—the Christian she had met four years earlier and had grown to love, though, she thought, perhaps only in a platonic way—had shown himself in many ways to be David's closest friend and confidant. But now—

She put her book down and looked appraisingly about the room. There was little of Christian in it, she thought. The books—there were several hundred of them in two large bookcases—were an eclectic assortment that, Christian had once told her, reflected his changing tastes, inclinations, and concerns over the years. If there was anything to tie them together it was a tendency toward the darkly philosophical—Camus, Kierkegaard, Sartre. But there was Mickey Spillane, too, and Sherlock Holmes.

Christian had no hobbies. He claimed that his work—his writing—was his hobby as well his profession. So there was nothing in the room to suggest a side of him other than his writing, although even that—he had authored nine books—was not much in evidence. There were several copies of his first novel—*Greed*—stuck in a lower corner of one of the bookcases, but all his other books were scattered about the house as if he didn't much care if anyone saw them. He didn't seem to take a lot of pride in what he did. He didn't talk about it, he shunned interviews with local news reporters, he was constantly invited to literary receptions and conventions, but rarely went. "Writing is simply a job," he said once.

He wrote about people falling in love, people falling out of love, about people who were in some long and ghastly process of dying. *Greed* had, in fact, encompassed all three areas, and had done it so successfully that the book had launched his career. But none of the books that followed had been as successful. Each had sold only marginally well. They had enabled him to make a living at writing, but he had not yet garnered any sort of real fame.

Karen thought that it was not a goal he hoped fervently to reach. She thought that he did not like people enough for it, or that he did not know himself well enough for it, did not feel that he had enough of substance to say.

He had told her as much. He had been half drunk and in a confessional mood: "Who am I to do calculations about other people?" he had asked. "I write about people and that means I write about myself. But when I look inward I don't see anything. Not myself. Not the reflection of myself. I see the dark." Then he had shrugged and said that he was babbling and quickly got onto another subject.

He read to her now and again from his own books. He seemed to enjoy it and she did not discourage him because he was a good reader—his voice full and deep and dramatic, almost Burtonesque. It was as if he were putting on a show for her, as if he were drawing, from somewhere deep within himself, living and breathing characters which, to that point, had existed only on paper.

His characters were often unlikable, seedy; he referred to them as "ne'er-do-wells," and explained that he had sympathy for them, even if many of his readers did not. It was, in large part, these characters which had kept him from gaining more popularity as a writer. "You know what these people are?" he once said to Karen, in his own defense. "These are the people that all of us want to be, under the skin. The properly dressed and courteous assholes that populate the world? *My* people live *inside* those people. You want to know why? Because from the moment we're born we realize, in our heart of hearts, that *other people* are in competition with us for survival. We act courteously, we dress properly, we smile, we say 'Have a nice day,' but it's all just to keep *them* at bay, to keep *them*—my people, the people inside us, the *naturalness* inside us—from gobbling us up."

He liked most to read from his first novel, *Greed*, the story of a love affair that was doomed because the people involved had let themselves become "too civilized . . . too polite," until, at last, the passion within them was gone and they realized it, mutually, and tried to correct it, at last, in an orgy of regret and violence. They had sacrificed their "real and gritty and passionate and natural" humanness for the sake of civility, out of self-loathing and fear, and in an effort to regain that humanness they self-destructed.

" 'Beverly looked at Stephen,' " he read, " 'and she saw a monster, something with a huge, misshapen head and bulbous eyes and a long, greedy tongue. She loved what she saw. *This* was her Stephen, and she knew that he was seeing her the same way, for the first time, and that he loved what he was seeing, too. Loved every repulsive, slavering, greedy, *human* part of her.

" 'Two monsters fucking. It was *real*, it was *good*, it would *last*.' "

And although these monsters were present only at the conclusion of his first novel, they filled all the pages of his succeeding novels, and they doomed him to a career that seemed always on the verge of getting started.

Karen decided she would like some coffee. She went into the small kitchen that adjoined the living room and put some water on to boil.

The dust which had gathered itself together and had become a man left the room and went out into the countryside. It was the beginning of a search. The man had no idea what he was searching for, only that he *needed* to search, and so he started.

There was light, and the countryside was still. There were smells in the air, and the man sniffed them and smiled because they were reminiscent, though he could not think what they were reminiscent of.

He was puzzled a little by the tug on him from above, by the fact that as he walked through the fields he could feel no pressure on the soles of his bare feet, only the softness of the earth beneath him and the slight touch and tickle of the grasses.

He was unaware of his nakedness because he had no idea that he should be clothed.

Eventually he came up over a rise and saw houses clustered together.

As he watched, people came out of the houses and ran to him smiling, and took him back to the cluster of houses, where he was clothed by many hands, welcomed, and caressed.

He had a meal. It too was reminiscent, though again he could not think what it was reminiscent of.

After the meal, darkness came and the people stayed inside their houses and they slept.

The man slept, too.

He dreamt of people he did not recognize.

He heard their names, but he did not know what the names meant.

He heard them talk, but did not recognize their voices.

He felt sadness.

When he woke, he had no recollection of the dream.

CHAPTER NINE

David was being held for observation in the psychiatric wing of Syracuse General Hospital. He'd been told it was standard procedure in cases of attempted suicide, and he hadn't argued with it. "Yes, you're right, of course," he said, which, calculatedly, seemed reasonable, because he wanted very much to seem reasonable, wanted very much to avoid being shut away in a locked ward.

He was not put in a locked ward. He assumed an appearance of being puzzled and remorseful at his "attempt at self-destruction," and so he was put in a room that was down a corridor which was looked after by a tall, middle-aged and very officious-looking RN who sat stiffly behind a desk.

There was a man sharing the room with David. The man was self-committed. He was depressed, and lonely, and was afraid of what he might do to himself. He talked to David quite a lot, and the idea David got was that the man not only despised his past, but lived in it, too. Hence his despair.

"So many faces, David," the man said. "So many names and faces and smells, and they all get crowded into here"—he pointed to his temple—"and they make me crazy."

David said, "I'm sorry," because it was clear that the man was in misery. The man was very thin because, he explained, food had not interested him in a long time; and his huge hazel eyes carried a constant look of sadness, though he smiled often. It was clearly a nervous smile.

The man explained, "There are aunts, uncles, cousins, David, and acquaintances, mothers, fathers, brothers, sisters. They all come and go in here." He pointed again at his head. "And even cats and dogs. Gerbils, too. And a parakeet who has no name. I remember them all. All of them, David. They're in here." He pointed. "They're gobbling away in here toward the inside of my skull and one of these days they're going to burst out."

David said again, "I'm sorry," but he had problems and needs of his own, and they were not being approached here, in the psychiatric wing of Syracuse General Hospital.

"Now there's you, too, David. *David.* You're in there with some other Davids. Half a dozen, I think. Like David Attenborough, the actor. He's in there, of course, because he was a part of my life—"

"Oh?"

"Well, yes, I saw him in the theaters, didn't I? And there's David, of David and Goliath—to say nothing of Goliath—and David O. Selznic, and David . . . David Ahl, who was my brother-in-law's friend, and David Letterman, and now you, too. David."

"It sounds like quite a crowd," David said, and

regretted the statement immediately, because he thought it sounded facetious, though it was merely the most appropos observation he could make at that moment.

But the man clearly did not consider the remark facetious. He gave David his nervous smile, his eyes sparkled a grim light; he said, "And I don't like crowds, David."

David tried to leave the ward that night.

He got into his clothes, left his room at a bit past eight, and walked quickly down the corridor toward the nurses' station, eyes on the nurse all the while. He smiled, nodded, was aware that she was watching him. She said, as he passed her desk, "Please don't leave us just yet, Mr. Case."

He stopped and pointed toward the closed glass doors. "I was going out for a bit. It's okay."

She shook her head. "No. I'm sorry. Please return to your room." He saw that she had her finger on a button on her desk.

"Orderlies?" he asked.

She nodded a little. David wasn't sure she was answering him or whether the nod was a nervous gesture. She said, "Please return to your room."

He looked for a long moment at the closed doors.

"Yes," the nurse said. "You could run."

He said, "I'm not going to do that. I don't need to do that." And he went back to his room.

In Anne's house, a breeze pushed in through the same window the martins had used and coaxed the pinkish white petals from a small flowering plant that had dehydrated.

In the basement of the house, the family of dormice set itself up in a corner far from the gas leak which had given the mother dormouse so much anguish.

At a little before nine, a cat got into the house through the open window. The cat was large and friendly and confused; earlier in the day, his owners had let him off on a country road not far off, then, with tearful eyes, had watched as their pet watched *them* drive away.

The cat's name was Jackson. His owners had thought it was an interesting cat name, one not on a list they had seen in a book about cats; it was a list of overused cat names, and Jackson's owners were intent upon being unique.

But Jackson was not unique. He was tired and hungry and confused. And he didn't know it, but no one would ever call him "Jackson" again.

Karen Duffy said to Christian Grieg, "I try to figure you out sometimes."

Christian said, "I didn't know I needed figuring out."

Karen nodded. "You do." A pause. "*I* need to figure you out." She smiled. She was aware that it was attractive and quietly sexual. "I guess I don't know if you mean well, Christian."

He smiled. It was designed to be understanding and forgiving. "You mean with you?" he said.

"With me?" she asked. "Our relationship?" She paused. "In a way. But that's not all of it—I was thinking," she hurried on, "when you were gone yesterday and I was waiting for you that I don't . . . know you very well." It was a gentle lie. She didn't know how to say to him, *I think you've changed in the last couple of months, Christian. I want to talk about it.*

"It's good that you don't know me very well," he said.

She thought a moment. "Yes. It's good. I see

what you're saying. But we don't have a *relationship*, per se. We *know* each other."

"I've always wanted a relationship with you, Karen."

She said nothing for a moment. If what he was saying was true, it was the first inkling she'd had of it. She said, "I wasn't aware of that."

"Weren't you?"

"No."

"You should have been. I was obvious about it."

"Then I was pretty dense, Christian. I'm sorry."

"That sounds like a brush-off."

She shook her head. "It isn't." She was confused. "I don't know what I want from you, Christian." She paused. "Because I really don't know you. I mean that." She wanted to add, *Especially lately*, but he said: "I have secrets. We all have secrets."

"I wasn't talking about that, Christian." There had been a tinge of anger in his voice and it concerned her. "I don't want to know your secrets." She was pleading with him and she wasn't sure why. "I want to know *you*, Christian."

He smiled; it came and went as swiftly as a heartbeat, but she knew it was a smile that she was not meant to see.

"Something's funny?" she said.

"Nothing's funny, Karen." He shook his head slightly. "Why?"

"Because you smiled."

"I didn't smile." Again he shook his head. "I'm sure I didn't smile." He looked upset.

Karen said, "I didn't mean anything by it, Christian. It was an observation. I thought you smiled."

He shook his head. "No. I didn't. I know when I smile."

"I'm sorry," Karen said.

* * *

A week after he was admitted to the psychiatric unit of Syracuse General Hospital, David was transferred to the intensive care wing; he was suffering from what appeared to be a drug-related relapse. He had slipped into unconsciousness, come back, slipped away again. Now, three hours after his initial unconsciousness, the monitor showing his brain function indicated that he was in a light coma.

David's doctor telephoned Laude Pharmaceuticals, talked with Kay Fortunato—David's lab assistant—told her the situation, and requested that she send him the results of all the company's research into A2d-40, including the results of human testing.

"There has never been any human testing," Kay told him.

"Never?" the doctor asked incredulously.

Kay said, "It was noted in the material I sent you when David was admitted a week ago."

"I haven't familiarized myself with that material."

"Doctor, I know that it arrived."

"Yes. It has. I've seen it, actually. I haven't studied it." He paused. "Miss Fortunato, if there has been no human testing then we've got a hell of a problem here."

Detective Fred Collins was inside Anne's house and he was spooked. Not just because it was a place where a murder had happened, but because he could so strongly sense Anne in it. Her personality. Her spirit.

He told himself that he did not believe in such things, that, actually, he *should not* believe in such things, because he had been in too many places where a murder had been committed and he was therefore jaded and professional. He had sensed before what he sensed here—spirit, personality, the leftovers of a person's existence—but it had always been fleeting and weak. It was not fleeting and weak, now.

Strangely, there seemed to be precious few leftovers of Anne Case here, although her house was full of furniture, books, paintings, art prints. Most of it seemed too much like window dressing—necessary accoutrements of a big house—that had little to do with the private and doomed personality that had lived inside it. There was little that was singularly reflective of Anne Case. There was a vase with flowers. The flower petals were on the floor and they were gray. (Collins smiled thinly at that. It was such a grim allegory.) On a table in the parlor there was a photograph of Anne—it was a small and oblong photograph that looked as though it had been cropped from a larger photograph. Collins had spent many minutes looking at it, but at last the face that smiled dimly back at him had told him little. It whispered of sensitivity and pain, but her life had screamed of it.

He had no reason for being in Anne Case's house today other than that he was intrigued by her. He thought that he might, when she was alive, have found good reason to love her.

It is several years earlier, the day after David's near drowning, and Anne—riding in Christian's car—has made the 120-mile trip from Batavia to the hospital in Syracuse, where David is recuperating nicely.

The trip has been hell for Anne. It's the first time in years that she's left her big, comfortable house for so protracted a time and when she arrives at the hospital, she feels ill—her stomach's churning, she's dizzy, seeing double.

Christian helps her from the car and, despite

her nausea, she hurries into the hospital, into the peace and security of finite spaces and unmoving walls.

And when she goes into David's private room, he gets shakily from his bed and hugs her.

The room is empty, except for the two of them. Christian has elected to wait in the lobby.

David whispers, "Anne, I went over."

She says nothing, though he assumes she's heard him.

"I went over to the other side, Anne," he whispers.

She nods. He can't tell the meaning of the nod. He moves back from her, holds her slim shoulders in his hands. He finds that he's smiling giddily. "You heard me, Anne?"

She nods, smiles too, and he's uncertain what kind of smile it is—a patient smile, a smile of assent, a smile of acceptance and belief. She's always been good at hiding her moods, when she wants, even from him.

David is still smiling giddily. He doesn't want to. He senses that, somehow, it's making his sister uncomfortable.

He sighs, forces his smile down. "Did I say thank you, Anne? For coming here?"

She looks silently at him for a few seconds. Then she tells him, her eyes still on his, "Let's not talk about what happened to you, David. It's . . . painful. Do you understand?"

He says nothing for a moment. He's not sure he understands. Is she talking about the accident itself, or about the fact that he went over to the other side? He wants her to explain. But he says, "Yes, I think so."

She shakes her head, smiling tearfully. "No," she says. "I doubt that you do." She nods at the bed. "Let's sit down, okay?"

"Okay," he says, and they sit together on the hospital bed, their bodies turned obliquely toward each other, hands clasped.

"Christian told me what happened to you, David." She takes a breath. "He told me what you believe happened to you."

"Do you doubt it, Anne?"

She shakes her head earnestly and looks down at their clasped hands. "No. God no!" She squeezes his hands. "I've thought quite often about dying." She pauses. "And about . . . going over." She looks up at him; she's still smiling tearfully. "We've talked about it, haven't we?" It's a rhetorical question. He doesn't answer. She continues, "And it's always been so . . . abstract." She pauses again. She touches his face tenderly. "Oh, David, you're all right, aren't you? They told me you were . . . under the water for a long time—"

He nods quickly. "Yes. I'm all right. The doctor says there should be no lasting effects."

"He said the same thing to me. I wanted to hear it from you, though. Doctors lie. They try to be kind, and they lie." She looks away, lets go of his hands. David wants to ask her what's troubling her, but says nothing. He knows that she'll tell him, in time.

She stands, goes to the window. The curtains are drawn. She reaches tentatively, hesitates, parts the curtain a little. Daylight shines on part of her face. She lets the curtain go, turns her head, looks at David. "Tell me what you saw there, David. On the other side."

He's confused by the question. He doesn't know where to begin, doesn't know where she *wants* him to begin. He says nothing, tries to formulate an answer, and while he's silent, Anne continues, "Is it a very *big* place? Is there lots of sky, David? Is there lots of *space*?"

He looks helplessly at her. He doesn't know what to say.

She continues, in a rush, "I imagine that there is. I've *always* imagined that there is. Lots of wide open spaces. A wide sky and open spaces." She pauses only briefly. "My God, my God!"

David goes to her, embraces her. "I don't know, Anne. It wasn't . . ." He pauses. "I don't remember," he lies. "I just don't remember."

She pushes away from him, looks into his eyes, and he can tell that she knows he's lying.

TEN

In Anne's house, Jackson found his way to the third floor, where the martins were; he didn't see them at first. But the martins saw him. After several minutes, one of the martins dive-bombed him, taking him by surprise. Jackson reared back and lashed out leadenly with one large paw. He couldn't do much with it. His erstwhile owners had had him declawed early in his kittenhood, but the instinct was still very much alive. Indeed, Jackson spent much of his time kneading the carpets or the edges of doorways in Anne's house, blissfully unaware that his claws were gone.

It was dusk when Jackson padded up to the third floor; this made him very cautious because, unlike most cats, his night vision was all but non-existent. The night frightened him. Since he had come here, the night had brought him dim recollections of the room at the house of his former owner; there had been a bright night-light in the room, and it had soothed him into sleep.

He squinted up at the martins. They were on a curtain rod high above him, at the top of a very tall window. They watched him squinting at them and, after a moment, the one that had dive-bombed him dive-bombed him again, again catching him by surprise, even though Jackson's eyes had been trained on them all the while.

The martins had decided, in their canny, bird way, that Jackson was different from other cats they had tangled with. He was slower. There was not the aura of death about him that hung so heavily around most other cats. So, they had decided that Jackson could be a source of fun.

Jackson, in his dim way, knew that the birds were not afraid of him. But this was all right, because night was falling rapidly, and as it fell, his fear rose. There were no night-lights in this house (he had looked), so the next best thing was a spot in a clothes closet where the walls on two sides of him and his awareness of the all but closed door in front of him gave reassurance that he was well hidden. Because of his night blindness, Jackson was an agoraphobic after dusk. He needed the comfort of walls and closeness. In daylight, it was very different. In daylight there were *possibilities*; there was movement, there were boundaries, there was color.

Jackson turned and trotted from the room where the martins were tormenting him. He went to the top of the stairs and looked down, toward the second floor, but he saw very little, only rectangular blacks and grays.

Something raked along his back. He whirled. He saw a swiftly moving shadow flit away, toward the room he had just left. He gave the shadow a confused, gurgling meow, then, because the light was failing quickly now, made his way to the closet on the second floor, where he would spend the night.

The martins followed him.

For David, it was not, now, a matter of sliding up through the tunnel, as if he were sliding *down* it on a stream of water. Now it was a struggle, a chore, and he felt a tug from behind; a rope might as well have been holding him, its strength not quite the match of his own. So he made progress, though in a slow and agonizing and dreamlike way.

Like a single bright star in the black fabric of the night, there was the mouth of the tunnel.

"Anne," he said, because it was the only name for him to rightfully say now.

"Anne."

He didn't *hear* his words so much as believe that he said them. But there was reassurance in that. Proof of himself. Proof of where he was and what he was and *that* he was.

Somewhere beyond his sight or caring a body lay still. Something random, deep in its bioelectronics, had made it stir occasionally, and had made it mutter words, names. But none of it made any more real sense than did the scratchings of chickens which might form letters in the dust.

He was not aware of the movements of his body as he made his way toward the mouth of the tunnel. He told himself that it was up, that he was climbing to it, but this was no more true than it would have been to say that the future was above him. It was *beyond* him and telling himself that it was *up*, that it was *above* him, merely gave him parameters. Because he knew what the tug from behind was. It was the earth. Mortality. It was the body in the bed.

Just as he told himself, too, that he was wearing

corduroy pants, white shirt, shoes. He was wearing nothing; nor was he naked. He formed for himself the image of his hands as he moved, the right
and left inward curves of his shoes as he moved.
He conjured up the sounds of his feet trudging
over hard earth. But there was no sound except
the whispers of his past.

He might have been floating, immersed. But that
would have had temperature, and he would have
felt a sense of motion, of being *inside*, as if in a
womb.

He could only *approach*, *will* himself closer, *be*
closer, *higher*, and, so, *closer* to that mouth. That
opening. *Into*. *Out of—*

The earth. The body in the bed.

Past blindness into sight.

It could have been days or no time at all that he
had been here. Only the body in the bed counted
such things and it was beyond counting. It
breathed. It perspired. It evacuated for its own
sake. It had taken over its own care. It counted
nothing. It was the *moment* that it lived. The *moment*. The inhale and the exhale but not the counting of it—the memory of it, and, so, the *naming* of
it.

The body in the bed named nothing. It had no
awareness of names; a wave does not call itself a
wave, nor did the body in the bed have a name for
itself.

It was the body in the bed that was, at *this moment*, an exhale, and, at *this moment*, an inhale.

Christian Grieg looked through the Plexiglas at
the body of his friend. It was lying very still.

Christian asked, "Would you say that he's close
to death?"

David's doctor answered, "No, sir. He's in a
coma. It's not deep. We expect that he'll come out

of it soon." The man spoke with a calm and practiced reassurance.

Karen Duffy asked, her eyes on David, though she turned her gaze to the doctor halfway through her question, "How long has he been like this?"

"Eighteen hours. Approximately eighteen hours," the doctor answered.

"But that's a very long time, isn't it?" Karen asked.

The doctor didn't answer at once. He seemed to be weighing his response. After several moments, he said, "Under some circumstances, yes. But not in his case. As I pointed out, the coma is very light. He has, in faet, shifted out of it momentarily. He's even spoken to us."

"Spoken?" Christian asked.

"A name," the doctor said. "His sister's name, I believe."

"Anne?" Christian asked.

The doctor nodded. "Yes. Anne. That's his sister? The one who was murdered recently?"

"Yes," Christian said. "Anne."

"A tragedy," said the doctor.

ELEVEN

It was easier now. The tug from behind was lighter, weaker, as if he were about to float. And the mouth of the tunnel, the opening, was ... nearer. In easy reach. He could reach for it, touch it.

He tried.

But the opening was no closer. It was at a distance. Above him, *beyond* him, as if it were a reflection in water. He reached for it again. He saw the image of his hand reaching and his hand was like white clay. Then there were veins on it, half moons, lines. It was a hand complete.

Christian Grieg said to Karen Duffy, "I always maintained that he was weak and this is proof of it."

David's doctor had just waddled off and disappeared left down a corridor, and now there were soft bells announcing that visiting hours were at an end in the nearby intensive care maternity wing.

Karen said, "I don't believe it; you *resent* him. I wouldn't have thought that that was possible, Christian."

Christian shook his head. He scowled. "I don't resent David. Why should I?"

Karen said, "I have no idea why, but it's what I just saw in you."

Christian smiled, It was flat and resentful and there was no humor in his eyes; they were hard and accusing. "You're *psychic*, Karen?" His smile vanished. "I didn't know that."

Karen looked at him a moment without expression. She shook her head. "I'm sorry. Clearly I've . . . touched a nerve—"

"That's an accusation, Karen. What are you accusing me of?"

She shook her head. She was confused; this was so unlike him—baiting her. She said nothing.

Christian said, "But we'll let it drop. I'm feeling magnanimous. My friend"—he nodded quickly to indicate the body in the bed—"is ill." He paused. "And I'm concerned."

It occurred to Detective Fred Collins that Anne Case had much the same effect on him that girls in high school—whom he had loved from afar and in vain—had once had; she intrigued him, she filled his mind and his senses. He imagined that he could *smell* her, not just in her house but around it, too, and then in his car as he drove off, and later, at his apartment, while he prepared for bed. As if she were lingering nearby, *watching* him, as if she found *him* intriguing and unapproachable.

It had been two weeks since her death and he had gone to her house three times, not including his initial visit, when he had seen her body, so many wounds in it, her face in peaceful repose. His logs noted each visit, and gave each visit a purpose—"Extension of on-scene investigation," one said—but he realized that his purpose was to know her from being where she had lived and died.

It was not the first time he had formed such an attachment, but it was the first time that it was so intense, and he fought it because it seemed morbid to him, and unproductive.

So he did not go into her house today. He looked at it from his car, looked at the white clapboards and green shutters, the red-tiled roof, the lawn that had grown tall. He looked past the yellow tape surrounding it; the tape read: POLICE LINE, DO NOT CROSS.

The house was sturdy and attractive; people would live in it, they would be told what had happened in it; at night they would pass through it from room to room, and they would imagine that there were shocking and remarkable things to see, if only they had the courage to look.

Fred Collins lingered with his gaze on the house for several minutes. His hand went to the car door handle once, and he gripped it as if he were ready to open it. But he stayed where he was. He was upset with himself, and confused; for being obsessed with a ghost; for creating for himself a woman to love out of the corpse of Anne Case and the leftovers of her life.

This house needs people in it, he thought, knowing that he was trying to distance himself from his purpose here.

At last, he drove off.

TWELVE

"**G**oing to be a beautiful day," said the voice.

David looked back. He saw a shadow, man-shaped, and behind it the pines, which were in great abundance here, and beyond the pines, wedges of pale blue sky. And above . . .

Above.

"No rain today," said the voice. "No darkness today."

Above.

"Today there is blue sky," said the voice. "Today is a beautiful day. All day."

David reached for the shadow of the man. He had no real idea why; perhaps he wanted to test this place, find its reality. But his arm was unfamiliar to him, white and straight—a piece of wood. Then there were muscles in it, then the skin was pink, and he recognized it.

But his arm was still a good distance from the

shadow of the man, and David's outstretched fingers touched only air.

He felt a breeze tickle the hair on his arms.

In awe, he whispered, "This is the earth."

The shadow of the man said, "Going to be a beautiful day. No dark today. Beautiful day."

David's arm dropped. He moved forward, closer to the shadow of the man. The man receded. The shadow receded. Its movement was attended by a low, flat rustling sound, like paper being crumpled. It was the sound of distance being established, David realized.

The shadow said aloud—louder, though still without urgency—"You can't stay. How can you stay?"

Then there was again the sound of paper being crumpled, and the shadow moved very quickly, as if it were the shadow of something very small that was being withdrawn by something very, very large. And so, in a moment, stillness was in the forest again, in the dust hanging in the air, in the silence.

At the house, dust collected, settled, formed, dissipated, collected again.

In the fields surrounding the house, people were picking fruit that grew on plants which hung close to the ground. The fruit was sweet, pungent, and red, like strawberries, and one of the people gathering the fruit straightened in the white light, held a piece of the fruit between his fingers, and smiled. "We could have whipped cream with this," he said.

There were people around him, but they made no acknowledgment of him. And the man, having already forgotten what he had said, popped the fruit into his mouth, enjoyed the squish of it under his tongue, and continued picking.

* * *

Christian Grieg and Karen Duffy had stayed at a motel outside Syracuse for the night following their visit with David, and they had made love. It was their first time; it had been awkward, self-conscious, unsure, and now, over breakfast at the motel's tiny restaurant, they were mutually embarrassed but did not want to show it.

Christian was thinking, as he and Karen talked, about the mistakes he had made in his life, the regrets he had fostered and sheltered now. This woman was one of those regrets, he had decided. He did not love her. How could he love her? She was like his sister, or his mother, so it would be wrong to love her in the way that he had.

"I'm sorry, Karen," he cut in.

She stopped talking. She had been talking about her work. "Sorry?" she said, not so he would repeat what he'd said, but because she simply hadn't heard him.

"I said nothing." He pushed a bit of scrambled egg around his plate. "Go on," meaning that she should go on talking about her work.

Karen mentally played back the last half minute. "You're sorry for last night, Christian? You needn't be."

A family came into the tiny restaurant. They were a family of four—mother, father, girl, boy—and they were all very fat. The father said in a high, squeaking voice to the mother, "Over there, Alice," and indicated a booth just behind the booth that Karen and Christian were in.

Christian glanced around at the family; he grimaced a little as they sat down, the man with his back to Christian, so the seat Christian was in moved and shifted. Christian looked around again. He said to the back of the fat man's head—which was covered with thin black hair—"Do you *mind*?"

The man did not respond.

Karen said, confused and embarrassed, "Christian?"

The fat man shifted in his seat, making room for his hefty wife. The wife said, "I don't have no room, Earl."

The two kids were pushing at each other now, not because they had no room but because they often pushed at each other. They smiled chubbily as they pushed; it was a game.

The fat man leaned forward to stop them then, and, when the kids quieted down for the moment, he leaned back with a *whump*.

Christian said again, "Do you *mind*?"

The fat man craned his small round head around and smiled at Christian. "Sorry?"

Christian hissed, "You're *moving* my seat, dammit!"

The fat man stopped smiling. His wife glanced critically at Christian, frowned, then looked at her children, who were again pushing at each other. As her husband had done, she reached across to separate them.

The fat man looked at his wife. "Let's move, Alice," he said. Alice nodded, and in a moment the family had seated themselves at a booth on the opposite side of the small room.

Karen said to Christian, "That was rude, Christian."

Christian said, "They were people to be rude to. Unnatural people."

Jackson found the window through which he had come into Anne's house and he stared confusedly at it from the floor. Finally, he leaped to the sill. He paused there, his four feet balancing him on the narrow sill, his big orange head bobbing, tail twitching. His tail twitched when he was in thought. For him, thought consisted of a series of almost random memories (pictures) that flitted through his brain. The memories were weighted plus and minus (though he did not consciously will this). One of the minus pictures which flashed through his head and vanished was of the night and the outdoors, and for Jackson that was blackness and noise and the touch of a thousand small creatures. The noise consisted of grunts, hoots, feet crunching the earth nearby. He had been outside at night only a few times, mostly as a kitten, and those times had formed for him a pulse of terror in the back of his cat brain, because although the hoots and the touch of a myriad of small creatures were disconcerting, the crunch of earth nearby told him that something very heavy was walking about, something his poor eyes could not see. And his only recourse was to run from the sound; run into blackness—into walls and trees, the tires of parked cars. So there really was no escape.

Except inside, into the light.

Which formed a plus memory. Being inside at night, his night-light guiding him safely into sleep.

There were other pluses and other minuses, all having to do with danger, safety, hunger, contentment; and they were mixed together in his cat brain so that *outside* did not necessarily translate as *danger*, and *inside* did not necessarily translate as safety and contentment.

So he balanced on the sill in Anne Case's house until, at last, some random pulse, like a spark, sent him leaping to the ground three feet below.

Above him, the window—its casing dried— slammed shut from the movement.

Jackson looked up. He meowed, mouth opening

wide in confusion, his poor eyes fixed on the closed window, tail twitching, cat brain racing.

He was out. The way in was shut. He *had* to be in.

He meowed pleadingly for a very long time at the closed window.

The body in the bed lay nearly as still as earth, shallow inhales and exhales marking slow time, and Death, waiting nearby, wanted so much to climb into the body, to still the breathing and make the body as cold and as motionless as stone. It was what reigned in the universe, cold and stillness. But Death couldn't climb into the body on the bed—its spirit was gone, was on an odyssey.

So Death stood by—and to all the eyes that watched, it looked much like the shadowed juncture of two walls, the straight line of Death.

THIRTEEN

Batavia was a small upstate New York city and Fred Collins—who had spent all of his adult life as one of its policemen, and had therefore passed a lot of time on its streets, watching its people—had a good eye for spotting the longtime Batavia resident, the visitor, the newcomer. He knew many Batavia residents by name, others simply by face or reputation.

He knew the patterns of their movements through the city within each month and season. He knew the drably dressed welfare mothers—usually with passive, obedient children in tow—the young singles, who seemed to breeze through the stores and malls, and then breeze out, back to their three-room apartments in one of the city's outlying apartment complexes; the transients, who—few though they were—were like transients everywhere; the young marrieds with infants strapped to their backs or belted into Perego strollers.

Fred Collins thought that he remembered Anne Case in the city, thought he remembered her moving quickly from store to store on that squat and white-walled main street, hugging close to the buildings, head down. And, in his memory, she was dressed as if to hide, even on that warm summer day, as if to be within the walls of her clothes.

But there was something good and childlike about her, he remembered (or thought he did), a warm and very appealing simplicity.

She would have been easy to pick out, easy to remember, even if he had seen her only once.

But he knew that he had never seen her until the day of her death, when there had been sixty-three stab wounds clustered around her stomach and back, and a look of peaceful repose in her eyes.

But he manufactured the memory, anyway, and thought it was good, thought that it comforted him.

He called to her in it, "Hello, Anne. Fine day."

But she did not stop as she moved quickly from one store to another on that squat street of white walls and storefronts. She merely turned her small, pretty face toward him, the glimmer of a smile and recognition came to her, and then was gone.

On the Other Side, there were cities that were both like and unlike other cities; they were places where people congregated. There were restaurants, museums, theaters, things nostalgic.

Wood predominated in these cities, but there was also brick—made from earth and water, baked in the light—and the roofs of the houses were tiled with flat stone. A panorama of the cities from some high point would have shown these flat stone roofs of various pitches and sizes, and the walls of many colors beneath.

Cars did not exist here, though people could occasionally be seen standing on corners, near the roadways—which were made of brick or flattened earth—with their arms outstretched. This behavior could continue for what would seem like a very long time to an observer from some other place.

In the museums there were artifacts on display which were in actuality manufactured things made from memories dulled by death and transition. There were replicas of washing machines, stereos, TV antennas, telephones and telephone booths, automobiles, floor lamps, children's toys of various kinds (teddy bears, rag dolls, building blocks, tricycles), guns, cameras. None of these items were functional. They were fashioned from various materials—stone, wood, earth, paper.

There were books here, too. They were written in longhand, in various languages, on paper made slowly and methodically by hand from wood pulp. The words and sentences in these books were fragmented and often unreadable except by the people who had written them. One such book, written in English, began:

Link own freon at the moreover blakness diskribing us. Sewwee rise UP! ! . . .

It went on, at very great length, to describe the effects of the Emancipation Proclamation as seen through the eyes of a young black man. In life, the author had been a white professor of history at Dartmouth College.

Another book, by a woman who had written fiction for various literary magazines, read, in part:

Arown that bed the Missusgathered wept
weree teres in vane; for the maen wus thair
dying inhis sleep;

He smild; he sayd to them awl, winking,
'Oh, I luvu.' Then he pastoff lykair; going up,
going up, lingering arown them his last em-
bras, tuching them with feengirrs madof
air. . . .

Which were the woman's jumbled memories of
her own death.

Painting and drawing were very popular here.
They were done in primitive, and very artistic,
polished ways, on handmade paper, on wood, on
walls, with paints made from flowers and grasses
ground in a mortar and pestle; drawings were
done with charcoal made from scorched wood.

All these things were reflective of memory. For
most of the people here, conscious memory was
nonexistent. Artists worked as if from some genetic memory that was incredibly strong but also
incredibly elusive. A *déjà vu* kind of memory.

And when David made his way through the still
forest, through the dust that hung motionless in
the air, through the tangy odor of pine tar, he
heard movement around him, as of bodies pushing gracefully through the dense foliage. And now
and again he saw a flash of color.

He experienced this as if he were experiencing
the landscape of a dream.

He felt no tug of gravity. He felt a pull from
above.

Above.

What he supposed were the leaves of a maple
tree were, on closer look, something else, something unrecognizable, something spikey and pale
green, with a tinge of orange or red at the center.

From this, he supposed that it was autumn.

* * *

Jackson could not find a way into Anne Case's house and it was nearly night. The house had many windows, but none were open, as he had discovered when he had leaped into one that was especially clean.

He had seen someone smiling pleasantly and invitingly at him from the window, and it had given him a good feeling, the kind of feeling he once had had when he heard the words, "Do you want to eat, Jackson?" and knew that his dinner was being served. But he did not think about it now, toward nightfall, and he would not think of it again. His memory was selective and defensive. He remembered the boy who had spoken to him. He remembered the car driving away. He remembered the thud of footfalls in the dark, the martins peering silently at him from their perch on the curtain rods in Anne Case's house. Those were memories that were real, things that had touched him, and had changed him. The smiling face in the window had been fleeting and had not touched him.

Because of a street lamp a hundred feet from the house, the front of the house was brighter than the back, and Jackson seated himself near the front door, so his dim shadow was cast on the stone walkway (inexplicably, the shadow gave him comfort), and he watched the front door. He gave a soft and pleading meow now and again because he sensed that he was being watched from within the house and that, sooner or later, the door would be opened for him.

But it was not. And, after a long while, Jackson wandered off.

BOOK TWO

A CREATURE TO RECKON WITH

ONE

I t is ten years later. Two people sit in the living room of what was once Anne Case's house. Their names are Maude and Peter. They're newly married and unsure of each other and of their lives together, which spread out before them like a desert.

But they tell each other that they are very much in love, and they believe it.

Maude says to Peter that she's not sure just how long they've been at the house.

Peter, who has the unfortunate habit of answering a question before it has been fully stated, answers, "Three weeks." He thinks and adds, "Twenty-three days, actually."

Maude asks if he likes being at the house.

"Yes," he says. "I like it."

She tells him that she's uncomfortable. She claims that there are "presences" in the house and reminds him of its history, about the murder ten years earlier.

Peter gives her a long-suffering smile because he has heard this sort of thing from Maude quite often in their relationship. She has claimed not only to have seen ghosts—when she was a child—but once to have spoken to one. She also proclaims that she's psychic.

He tells her now, "There are no ghosts in the house, Maude."

She tells him that she isn't so sure of that.

"Because, very simply," Peter explains, "there are no ghosts," and he gives her a soft half smile which begs her forgiveness for being rational.

Maude smiles back her forgiveness. "I've heard screams," she says.

"I haven't," Peter says, his words overlapping hers slightly.

"You aren't here when I am."

Peter says nothing.

Maude continues, looking away from him, "During the day."

Peter nods slowly, as if he's thinking about this. Then he says, "Have you heard these screams at any particular time?"

Maude shakes her head. "Not really. The afternoon."

"What time in the afternoon?"

Maude shrugs. "Late, usually. Shortly before you get home."

"And are they loud, these screams?"

Maude shakes her head. "Not very."

Peter smiles. "But loud enough?"

She nods. "Loud enough to hear, yes."

Peter's smile grows a bit broader. "And it's someone in the house, you think?"

"Not some*one*, some*thing*!"

"Of course. Some*thing*."

She eyes him suspiciously. "You find this very amusing, don't you?"

He shakes his head earnestly. "I would never laugh at you, darling. Never. I'm a little *amused* by what you're saying, I think. Can you blame me? If there's someone screaming in the house late in the afternoons, if the place is haunted, then what in the hell are we still doing here?"

"We're here because she needs me."

"She?"

"The woman who screams. The woman who was murdered here."

"Oh. Does she have a name?"

"I don't remember her name. But what does that matter?" She hesitates. "It *doesn't* matter."

Maude and Peter are sitting side by side as they talk. Occasionally, she looks at him or he looks at her; both believe they have the full measure of the other. Peter believes that Maude is touting her "sensitivity," and Maude believes that Peter is taking the pose of the "rational man" (as always). She's amused by it, so she keeps him talking. She says, "Names don't matter."

"For ladies who scream in the afternoon it does," he says, and his eyes sparkle as if to say that it was a wonderful comment.

Maude suppresses a smile. She suspects that he is very pleased with himself.

He confirms her suspicion: "That was a good thing to say wasn't it? 'For ladies who scream in the afternoon it does.' It was kind of . . . pithy and . . . theatrical."

"Very," she says, without looking at him.

Peter looks silently at her a moment. His mouth twitches a little; clearly he's on the verge of some critical remark. But he looks away and says, "The lady's name was Anne . . . something."

"Anne Case," Maude says, because the name has just come to her.

"It's a strong name," he says, "in a feminine way." He gives her a puzzled look. "Did you understand that?"

"A strong name," she says. Then, "Yes, I understood." She looks away. "I see her drifting about in this big house, all alone. It's very tragic. Very tragic. To be strangled in one's own house. One's own sanctuary. Then left alone in it . . . to . . . wander about in the place of your own murder for all eternity."

"I believe that she was stabbed," Peter says.

"No. I'm sure she was strangled," Maude says. "Strangled. And left to linger here forever."

Peter says nothing for a moment. Then: "Do you really think that's what happened to her? That she's in some kind of limbo in this house? For all eternity?"

She shrugs. "Of course. What else is there?"

He shrugs. "Nothing, I guess."

Fred Collins passed Anne's house three times on the Saturday two weeks after her murder. He had stopped trying to rationalize this behavior by telling himself it was only a part of his work. He knew that it was something beyond that. He knew that he was in love with the woman he supposed she had been—in love with her vulnerability, with her illness, with her strength (for putting up with what life had thrown at her, after all). He would have wanted to protect her, he knew; there was no getting around that fact, unseemly as it might have appeared to some. But, beyond that, there was the inescapable truth that she was earthy and wise within her frailty. She had suffered under enormous pain (the pain of her illness) from day to day, and so it could not be otherwise.

And now, in these past two weeks, she was suffering under a very different but incredibly more immense kind of pain. But ironically, perhaps there was something he could do about it.

Perhaps his love and attention could ease it.

Nineteen years before her death, Anne Case is sitting with her twin brother, David, in their parents' house and they're discussing what—she does not then realize—are the beginnings of her illness. Its onset. Occasionally, she glances out the window at the snow-covered street as they talk. Her oval, pleasant face and gray eyes are expressive and changeable from one moment to another; mostly, they're expressive of sadness, and this confuses her brother. At sixteen, he can't understand what his twin sister would have to be sad about.

"I get scared sometimes, David," she says, and her eyes flit to the window, then to her brother's face. She grins a little, as if embarrassed, and looks away.

David says, "Scared a what?" and grins too, though she's no longer looking at him. His gaze settles on a soft blue vein which is just barely visible beneath her cheek. The color of the vein surprises him.

She says, eyes averted, "Things."

"You're scared a things? What things?"

She shrugs; her eyes are still turned away. His eyes are still on the blue vein in her cheek. "Lots of things. Most things."

"You scared a *me*, Anne?"

She shakes her head quickly, glances at him, grins, looks away. "No, David. Just things. Most things."

"Scared how?"

She gives him a puzzled look, then it's apparent

that she understands. "David, I get nervous. I get scared, like . . . when we're riding in the car and Dad's driving too fast. Like that." A quick smile creases her lips, then as quickly is gone, as if she's pleased with her analogy, but is also saddened by what it conveys.

David shakes his head. "But you're not always ridin' in the car, Annie."

She shakes her head, frowning. "You don't understand—"

But suddenly, he does understand, and he's embarrassed by his apparent thickheadedness. He nods quickly. "Yes I do. I know what you mean, I know what you mean." But he doesn't elaborate on it; there is no need. He asks her, "Why, Annie?"

"I don't know," she whispers. "And that scares me, too."

"Gee, there sure are a lot of things that scare you!" It is meant as a joke, but as soon as it comes out, David realizes that it's cruel, so he apologizes quickly, and adds, "I wish I could help you, Sis. I can see when you're scared. You look like you think someone's gonna hit you."

"It's how I feel, David."

"Yeah." He nods. "I know." *Know what?* he asks himself. "I know," he repeats, and pats her hand. Her fingers curl over his hand. A quivering smile comes to him. He says, "You'll be okay, Sis. It's just . . . growing up is all."

She says nothing. She grips his hand very tightly.

Christian Grieg sat alone in his house and wondered why Karen Duffy had fallen in love with him, and why he had let her do it. He thought that he could have stopped it. He thought that he knew the reasons why people fell in love, why *she* had fallen in love with *him*; and the fact was that she hadn't. Not really. She thought she had. Everyone *believed* in love, in falling in love, in *being* in love, but it was no more real or reliable an emotion than superstition. (And, in a strange way, it was unnatural, too. Did animals "fall in love"? No. They mated. They produced babies. But they didn't trip all over themselves about "falling in love.")

Karen loved him because she thought she understood him, she supposed that she saw a chink in his armor, a tear in his facade of strength and stability. So she wanted to *mother* him. She saw *weakness* in him and wanted to protect him from it—and, with her love and affection, soften the blows of a hurting and uncaring world (which, also seeing his weakness, would take advantage of it).

She probably even imagined that she knew him better than he knew himself. The newly-in-love always imagined such things, always supposed that they had been allowed a glimpse of *real* humanness, which is real *weakness*.

He took a drag of his cigarette. After five years, he had begun smoking again, and though he was repulsed by it, he accepted that he needed it, so he smoked with great satisfaction, drawing the smoke in very slowly and deeply and letting it out in great gray clouds through his nose and mouth. It had made him dizzy at first, but that had passed.

He knew that Karen hoped he was in love with her. It was obvious. No one says "I love you" without expecting reciprocation. So he'd said it. It was the kind thing to do.

He wished now, as he sat alone and smoked and remembered his kind deception, that he was not the person that he was. He wished he were younger, a child, when most of his decisions had been made for him, when he had not had to make

the kinds of decisions that circumstances forced
him to make now. He wished he were ten or twelve
years old again. He was someone he liked, then.
He hadn't even thought about whether he liked
himself or not. But he thought about it now,
twenty-five years later, and he knew it was true.
He had liked himself. And now he liked the child
he had been. He guessed it was that way with everyone—with Karen, and even with David, who lay
quietly dying. We become people we despise,
Christian thought, because we grow into adult-
hood, and independence, and that changes us—
necessarily and regretfully—into people who have
to hurt other people in order to survive and re-
main independent.

Who can really love the grasping and desperate
and hurtful adult?

Who can despise the guileless and dependent
child?

He realized at once that Karen loved the child
in him. He smiled. He enjoyed the revelation.

The cigarette he was holding had burned down
to a nub that burned the insides of his fingers. He
stared at the nub for a moment, aware of the hot
pain it was causing, but slow to react to it. He
thought briefly that there was importance in the
fact of his slow reaction. He thought that some
change was taking place inside him. A metamor-
phosis. It would be truly fascinating to witness.

He stubbed the cigarette out in the ashtray near
his chair.

It is the morning of Anne's murder. There is
bright sun and warmth. Inside her house, Anne
Case is humming. She's unaware of it. Her humming is low and sweet sounding, though the tune
is unrecognizable, borrowed from bits of this tune

and that tune, until it becomes a tune of her own making.

She's watering plants. She has Dracena, Boston Fern, Diffenbachia, Croton, Sheffelliera, and they are all around the house, several dozen of them within the house's fourteen rooms, though there are now none in the third floor ballroom; the room has begun to make her very uncomfortable in the past couple of weeks. It is the room where the rape happened.

Anne is thinking about the rape as she hums. Not the rape itself, not the physical act of penetration and violence that the man perpetrated on her, but the surprise of finding him there, in that room. She keeps her house locked. She thought she knew the house, its moods, its movements; she thought that the house spoke to her in its way, and she was surprised when she saw the form in the corner, across the big room. The man waiting with his arms folded.

The light on him was suggestive—light from the window, from the spotlamp on the front of the house. Light that was reflected and refracted up from below, through the window, off a mirror, and then in a narrow rectangle onto the man's crotch, which was what she focused on first. Not his face. Because she knew he intended rape. She knew him, and she knew that it was what he wanted—to violate her. To give her fear and pain.

She realizes that she's humming as she remembers. She stops humming. The humming offends her. It's an impropriety. Like laughing at a graveside.

The morning's light and warmth has begun to heat her house up. Reluctantly, she goes to a window nearby to open it. She finds that it's unlocked. She tries to remember if she locked it and tells herself that of course she locked it because she locks all the windows in her house and she keeps them locked. But she could have unlocked it. The day before she could have unlocked it because it was hot then, as it promises to be today. But she does not remember unlocking it.

It occurs to her all at once that there is someone else in the house, that the house is talking to her and telling her that there's an intruder. She chooses to believe this but not to act upon it. Acting upon it would be an admission of trouble this bright warm morning and she does not want to admit there is trouble until she has real proof.

She's a tall, thin woman, graceful and pleasant looking, and the man watching her thinks that she is deserving of rape simply because she *is* so pleasant looking, so graceful, so nearly ethereal. People aren't supposed to be that way. People are clods. People are clumsy. People snort and belch and fall down. That is the way God intended them to be. And it is not the way this woman is. People were not meant to be like the animals—graceful and ethereal. Animals never thought about themselves or about their place in the universe. They simply *were*. They simply existed. And they obeyed the dictates of their genetic predispositions.

Just as he is doing.

Anne begins to hum again. She's downstairs, near the locked door to the cellar, which is just off the expansive and well-furnished kitchen. She's aware of the smell of olive oil from the butcher block table in the center of the kitchen, left over from a meal the night before that she shared with her brother. She's very aware of smells; all her senses are keen. (*"Sometimes, David,"* she said a long time ago to her brother, as if in awe, *"I think that I hear too well, and that I see too well. And it's like I'm being ... bombarded by the world around me."* She gave him a quizzical look. *"Do you understand that?"*

("Sure, Annie," he answered, though it was not entirely the truth—he understood only her words; it would be years before he understood their importance.)

And now she smells something else lingering beneath the smell of olive oil. She smells nervous sweat.

To her right and left a hallway leads—right—to the library, which is filled, floor to ceiling, with books that are often picked over; and—left—to the huge living room, where a grandfather clock strikes the quarter hour. There's a boot closet ten feet from her. It's from this closet that the man watches. He has the door opened a crack, though he's unconcerned, now, whether she sees him.

He has been in the house throughout the night. He's picked over some of the books in the library, and returned them to the shelves (upbringing). He has prepared a light breakfast of Wheaties and orange juice and has put his dishes in the dishwasher afterwards (upbringing). He has stood silently in Anne Case's bedroom and watched her sleep, her face illuminated softly by the spotlamp on the wall below her bedroom. He has thought desperately of pulling her blankets down as she sleeps (lust).

But he needs to do violence to her and that is far more powerful within him than his lust. He wants to overcome her, to overcome her beauty, her serenity, her security here in her big house. He wants to show her that he has power and that she is powerless in the face of it.

He pushes the boot-closet door open.

She does not react. Her head stays down. She's intent on a Dracena, she seems to be examining

one of its leaves as she hums. The leaf is brown
at the edges.

He reaches and pushes the open door hard so it
slams against the wall. He sees her flinch, but that
is all. She does not look up.

He whispers to her—in a voice that hisses and
carries the promise of violence in it—"Hello,
Anne." He pauses only a short moment. "I think
you were expecting me."

She does not react. Her attention apparently remains fixed on the Dracena's dying leaf. This confuses him. He watches her a moment. Has she
gone deaf in the last week? he wonders. No. She
flinched! She *did* hear him.

He pushes the closet door again. And again it
slams against the wall. She does not flinch.

He has a small knife in his pocket and he pulls
it out and holds it up in front of his face. The knife
has a blade that's dull from too much polishing
so it looks like pewter. But he conjures up the
idea that the knife glistens in the morning sunlight slanting through a nearby window.

He tells her, again in his hissing, violent whisper,
"I have a knife, Anne."

She does not react.

His confusion is giving way to anger. He believes that she's playing a game with him.

"You're toying with me, my sweet," he says. She
does not react. Her attention apparently remains
fixed on the Dracena and its heavy dying leaf. He
growls, "Don't toy with me!"

She turns a little, so her back is to him. She's
dressed in a long gray dress that hangs nicely on
her.

He steps out of the closet, still holding his small
dull knife in front of him. He stops after a few
steps. His breathing is very heavy and quick,
though from anger and confusion rather than an-

ticipation. He wants to speak to her but he isn't sure what to say. He wants her acknowledgment, wants proof of her fear and of his mastery of her, because he's certain she's toying with him.

He takes several steps. Stops. He is still holding the small dull knife in front of his face and for a moment he's aware that he must look very foolish. The moment is gone.

He says, "And what if I told you that I loved you, Anne?" He's very surprised by this and unsure of where it comes from.

Suddenly he's filled with anger. He rushes at Anne and plunges the dull blade into her back.

He did not intend his first blow to be so accurate, and for several moments he's not entirely aware of its accuracy. He watches Anne fall face forward onto the oak floor, so her head is turned to the right—he sees that her eyes are closed—and her arms are at her sides, left palm down, right palm out. Her legs are together.

He stares at her. He realizes that his first blow has killed her, but he does not admit it at once. He didn't want his first blow to kill her. It's why he chose such a small knife. He wanted her to endure many blows.

"*Damn* you!" he hisses.

He falls to his knees so her legs are between his legs. He is enraged. She must react, must react!

He raises the small dull knife high over his head and brings it down.

He does it again.

And again.

And again.

The earth. The body on the tile floor.
Past blindness into sight.
It could have been days or no time at all that she had been here. Only the body on the tile floor

counted such things and it was beyond counting. It did not breathe. Or perspire. It no longer cared for itself. It counted nothing. It was the moment that it died. The moment. The inhale and the exhale and then the stillness, but not the counting of it—the memory of it, and, so, the naming of it:

The body on the tile floor named nothing. It had no awareness of names—a wave does not call itself a wave, nor did the body on the tile floor have a name for itself.

It was the body on the tile floor that was, at this moment, an exhale, and, at this moment, stillness.

TWO

One of the nurses monitoring David outside his room in Intensive Care noticed a change in his respiration and EEG. She paged David's doctor, who was in the middle of a shower but heard the paging anyway. Five minutes later he was beside David's bed, his legs and bottom still damp from the shower. He scowled at the dampness.

David's eyes flickered open. Closed.

The doctor leaned over him. "Mr. Case?" he whispered. "David?"

No reaction.

The nurse monitoring outside the room said into her microphone, "His respiration is becoming shallow again, Doctor."

"Dammit!" the doctor whispered. "David!" he said sharply.

David's eyes popped open.

"Respiration heavier," the nurse said into her microphone.

"David?" said the doctor. "Can you hear me? Blink if you can hear me."

No reaction.

The doctor shone the beam of a penlight into David's eyes, found the pupils responsive.

David turned his head ever so slightly toward the doctor. It was a quick and unexpected motion, and the doctor straightened a little in surprise. He grinned, embarrassed, and leaned over once more. "Mr. Case? Are you with us?"

No reaction.

"Mr. Case?"

David turned his head so he was once again staring at the ceiling. "My God," he whispered, "I'm back."

THE FOLLOWING DAY

"He'll tell you a wild story," the doctor said to Christian Grieg and Karen Duffy, seated in front of his desk. "He'll tell you he's gone over to the other side." He shrugged. "Heaven, as it were—"

"No," Christian interrupted. "He'd object to that."

"Object?" The doctor was puzzled.

"To your characterization of this . . . place he claims to have gone to as 'heaven.' He'd disagree with it."

Again the doctor shrugged. "Be that as it may— and I really fail to see the difference; the difference is actually just one of semantics, isn't it? Be that as it may," he repeated, "we are going to hold him for a few more days."

"Why?" Karen asked.

The doctor shook his head a little as if in reassurance. "Observation. Merely observation, Miss Duffy." He paused meaningfully. "And there really is no assurance that he won't try it again, is there?"

"Try 'it'?" Karen asked. "Try what?"

"Suicide," the doctor said.

Karen gave him a tight smile. "You can't hold him forever."

Christian said, "Perhaps it would be better for David if they did."

The doctor stood. He said to Christian, "But that's out of the question, of course."

Christian nodded vaguely.

The doctor came around the desk, went to the door, opened it. "If you'd follow me, please. I'll take you to Mr. Case."

David's memories were as vivid as pain, as vivid and as real as the bed he lay in or the smell of anesthetic that hung in the air like a mist. And precisely because his memories were so vivid, he found it very hard to believe them. Memories were always dulled by present events, and by the expectation of future events; they got filed in a mental storehouse where they could be pulled out now and again. And they were never as vivid and as real as these memories were.

These could easily have taken form and shared the room with him, as if they weren't memories at all but a reality that existed outside the scope of his five senses.

No. He could *smell* pine tar. Dust.

"Back with us," he heard. He turned his head toward the door to his room. Christian was there, grinning what looked like a mock-friendly grin. Karen was beside him. She looked concerned, David thought. The doctor was already in the room.

Karen said, "You're going to be all right, David.

You had a bad time, but now you're going to be all right."

The doctor said, "How are you feeling, Mr. Case? Do you think you're up to visitors?"

No, I'm not, David thought. He turned his head so he was looking at the ceiling. He nodded. "Yeah, sure," he said.

There was a moment's silence. Then Christian said, "So tell us all about it, David. We're here because we're your friends. But you know that, of course." David thought he could hear sarcasm in Christian's voice. He turned his head. Christian was grinning very slightly, as if remembering something that gave him secret pleasure. David turned his head so he was looking at the ceiling.

"Yes," he said, and felt suddenly bone weary, as if sleep were going to overtake him. But it didn't.

They asked him questions.

"How are you feeling, David? Are you still depressed?"

"No. I was never depressed. Not in the way you imagine."

"What does that mean? Depression's depression—especially if it makes you suicidal. It's something to deal with, something to overcome—"

"Don't badger him, please," the doctor warned.

"Who's badgering? I'm concerned. I'm the man's friend, for God's sake!"

David listened and answered, "It was not suicide that I attempted."

"Of course it wasn't," Karen interjected.

"So maternal," Christian said. Then, "Was it the same place, David? The same place you went to five years ago?"

David shook his head. "I don't know." He paused. "Yes. The same place."

"But you went . . . deeper?"

David nodded. "Deeper," he whispered. "Yes."

"How much deeper?"

"He's tiring," the doctor warned.

"It was a simple question."

"Not so simple," David managed.

"It's the heart of simplicity, David."

"Deep," he said.

"And you're going to try it again, aren't you?'

"No. Of course not."

"We're not convinced, David." Christian's voice.

A pause; then, "I need answers. I have no answers."

"What sort of answers?" Christian asked.

"Answers to . . . questions I have. We've talked about this already."

"Questions about Anne?" Christian again.

"Yes. Mostly."

"I'm afraid that I must insist now—"

"What do you need to know, David? We know what's important. We know who killed her."

"Possibly. I don't know. I thought I knew, but I'm not sure."

"Please, no more questions. Your friend is very tired."

"We really *do* know who killed her, David. So what else do we need to know?"

David said nothing and, a minute later, Christian and Karen were gone and he was alone.

But he knew that he was not alone. He knew that something had come into the room with them, and had stayed, and still lurked in their absence.

He glanced about the room, expecting to see more than beige walls, monitoring equipment, gray blankets.

And he did.

He saw dust.

He smelled pine tar.

And he heard distant voices raised in gaiety.

Then he slept.

IN BATAVIA—THE FOLLOWING MORNING

Leo Kenner said, "Our boy did the rape. Are we agreed on that?" During Anne's autopsy, it had been discovered—through bruising on her shoulders and arms and around her pelvic area—that she had very probably been raped.

"Our boy?" said Fred Collins.

"Brian Fisher. We agree that he did it, right?"

"The medical examiner wasn't certain it was rape. It was just a guess."

Kenner looked suddenly exasperated. He fished for a moment in the thin file on Anne Case's murder—it lay open on his desk—then handed a page from it across to Collins.

Collins glanced quickly at it. It was page one of the Genesee County medical examiner's *Report of Autopsy*. At the bottom of the page, outlined in red pencil, were the words, "The high probability exists that subject was victim of forced intercourse one week–ten days prior to death. . . ."

"So?" Kenner coaxed.

Collins handed the sheet back. "If she *was* raped, then I'll concede that Fisher probably did it. But it doesn't jive with his profile—"

"That profile was done postmortem. What use is it? He killed *himself*, he killed *her*, so of course he raped her. What could be clearer?" It was to Kenner's credit that his pointed questions were clearly not rhetorical.

"Of course it's clear, Leo," Collins said. "I simply don't believe it." He shrugged. "And for me, that throws a monkey wrench into our whole investigation. If Brian Fisher didn't rape her, who the hell did?"

"Uh-huh. Well, I believe that he did rape her. But the point is, Fred, even if he didn't, then the bald and unattractive fact remains that he did indeed *kill* her, and that's what we're interested in here. Am I right?"

Collins said nothing.

It is ten years later and Maude and Peter are talking, filling the air with chitchat that is better than discussing their love life, which has become nonexistent in the last few weeks, though neither can pinpoint why.

Maude says, in answer to a question Peter asked her hours before, "No, they never really found her murderer." She turns her back to Peter so she can put on a blue negligee. She believes that his eyes are on her, and she resents it.

From the bed, with the blankets pulled up to his chin against the cold, early winter night, Peter says, "Someone confessed. I was talking to Lynn today"—the house's previous owner; she's holding the mortgage and keeps in regular touch—"and she said that someone confessed."

"I know that." Maude turns, faces him.

"You look very nice," Peter says, and smiles appreciatively.

"Thanks," she whispers, as if not wanting to acknowledge his remark.

"Really," he says with enthusiasm. "You look very fetching. Do you wear that every night?" He pauses, though not long enough for her to answer, then goes on, frowning a little, "Yes, I guess you do."

She nods slightly, as if embarrassed. She indicates the negligee. "It's getting too cold for this thing."

"I'll keep you warm," he says with a leer.

"Sure, thanks," she says without enthusiasm, and comes to bed, climbs in next to him, but lays on her back and puts her hands behind her head. "I still hear her," she says.

"Our ghost?" he says.

She nods.

"Same time, same place?" He grins.

She looks sharply at him. "Don't joke about it. Please."

He looks at her a moment, decides she's being serious, then says, "Sorry. It's just that I've never heard her—"

"So you think I'm crazy?"

"No." Silence.

"That was a very unconvincing negative, Peter." Silence.

She glances at him. His gaze is on the ceiling. She says his name. He looks at her, grins. "Let's make love," he says.

She looks away. "I can't. I'm sorry."

He sighs loudly. "Can you give me a reason?"

"Do I need to?"

"I asked for one."

A short pause, then, "I don't have one, I guess." Another pause. "I'm just not in the mood."

"Headache?"

"No."

"Maybe you don't find me attractive anymore?"

"No."

"No?"

"Yes, I find you attractive—"

"It's *her*, isn't it? It's your ghost."

Silence.

"She's made you . . . shy, or something."

"That's absurd."

Peter shakes his head quickly. "I understand now. I understand completely. You think she's *watching* us." He smiles, though he realizes it's a mistake; he can't help himself. "You think some woman who was murdered *ten years ago* is going to watch us making love so you . . . just *don't* make love. My God, my God, that's—"

"She was murdered *here*, dammit. In this house. In this very *room*, for all we know—"

"Not true. She was murdered downstairs. That's what Lynn told me."

"Oh, fuck Lynn!"

"I may have to." Peter closes his eyes. He's put his foot in it now, he realizes. He whispers, eyes still closed. "Sorry. That was stupid."

Silence.

He looks at Maude. She's crying softly. He sighs. "Really," he says. "I didn't mean it. It was a real, real stupid thing to say."

Maude shakes her head.

"That's not why you're crying?" Peter guesses.

Maude nods. She manages, "I'm crying because of her."

"Lynn?"

"No, for God's sake! Will you shut *up* about her. I'm talking about Anne Case. I . . . feel her in the house. I feel that she is very sad, and that she needs someone. A friend."

"You?"

Maude shakes her head. "I couldn't, even if I wanted." A pause. "And I *do* want—"

"Now you're spooking me."

She says, as if in sudden revelation, "Let's make love. Now. Right now!"

Peter pulls back from her. His brow furrows. "What an invitation to a hard-on."

"But . . . I mean it. Let's make love. You don't want to make love?"

"Of course I do. But not because you think your . . . friend is going to be watching. Not to show her you sympathize, or that you understand, or that you're willing to share me with her—"

"That's disgusting! That's repulsive! How can you talk like that? How can I make love to someone who talks like that?"

"Maude," he says, "you're sounding very unlevelheaded."

She says nothing for a moment. She wants to say, *You mean, I sound* female *right*? but she's not sure which way that will take them, or the discussion. She's trying to steer the discussion, and she knows it. She says, "I don't mean to sound that way." She pauses, adds, "Some of what you say has merit."

"Some of it?"

"Most of it." Another pause. "All of it."

Now Peter's amused. "You're kidding. You wanted to *share* me with a ghost just to show her you could be her friend?" He smiles. The smile becomes a quick chuckle.

Maude says, "I didn't realize it until you brought it up."

"It's incredible. It sounds like a *National Enquirer* headline: *Woman Shares Husband with Ghost*. It's a hoot."

"Please. You're being unkind."

"To her?"

"Who else?"

"Darling, she does not exist. You may not believe that, but it's regrettably true."

Maude says nothing. She knows that Peter will come around sooner or later.

They don't make love that night.

THREE

The middle-aged woman who wrote of her own death couldn't get it right because part of her was still bound to the earth and so she looked at death incorrectly.

"The missusgathered," she wrote, "and wept weeree teers invane for the maen lying ded."

What she saw with the misted eye of her memory was the end of existence. She saw a body being shuffled into the ground and dirt thrown over it and decay starting.

She wrote, "And he had ben a goudman, yes, and thair were meneechildren left two weepand remember."

As if it were a dream, she disguised herself from herself by changing her sex and her marital status (for in life she had been divorced, without children).

Only sometimes, when she looked back, she saw

a silver thread rising up from the man's body; she wrote of it, "Thenthe spidersthair were hard at wirk awl atonce tieing himup,"although this characterization annoyed her and made her feel that she was being dishonest, though she couldn't imagine why.

When she slept, she dreamt of her previous life, of the man she had loved then, of her mother, of a niece she had cared for. She walked with these people in her dreams, or she caressed them, or talked with them of the things which had once concerned her. And when she woke she remembered snippets of these dreams, the quick glimpse of a face, a smell that came and went as quickly as the beat of a wing. She told herself—as did many people here who had had similar dreams— that these were visions of things to come, people yet to arrive, situations not yet formed; "those on the horizon," they were called.

There were names in her dreams, too. She remembered some of them clearly. Rebecca, Mark, Jason. Like many others, she mouthed the names from her dreams often. She whispered them under her breath, sang them, said them aloud at odd moments, surprising herself with them, as if they had escaped, unbidden, from within her. And like the others here, she had no idea what names were for. She knew only that when she said them, they brought her a feeling of happiness, or sadness or, sometimes, a feeling of deep closeness that made her skin tingle.

Her father was here, though he was not nearby. He was in one of the cities. And she saw him, too, in her dreams, though distantly; in her previous life, she had known him only a little. He had died when she was just starting school.

She wrote, "The missusgathered wept weery

teers for the woman, buthey needant." She reread it and wondered about it. It spoke some truth to her, she realized, but it was a prickly and uncomfortable truth because she could not get hold of it. She stared at what she had written for a long time, trying to fathom it.

Elsewhere, others were doing similar things. Some who painted, some who wrote music, or sculpted, or wrote—all in answer to a great need within them—stepped back from their creations and wondered at them, heard the whisper of new truth in them, but could not hear it well enough to make sense of it.

But this did not happen to everyone. And when it happened, it was like the unexplained passing of a chill through the body (when it is said, perhaps, that someone has "just walked over my grave").

David knew that he was going to go back. He knew also that he'd have no trouble getting there.

It was here with him even now, in this hospital room—the smell of pine tar and dust and the distant sound of happy voices.

He'd have no trouble getting back.

It was nearly as simple as . . . stepping over.

("David Case?"

"Yes. Who is this?"

"My name is Leo Kenner. I'm a detective with the Homicide Division of the Batavia Police Department. Sir, do you have a sister named Anne Case?"

"I do. She lives in Batavia. She's fine."

"I'm very sorry, Mr. Case, but—"

"She's *fine*, I told you! I spoke with her very recently. I know what you're going to tell me.

You're going to tell me that something's happened
to her. Some . . . accident. You're going to tell me
that she's hurt. But you're wrong."

"I'm very sorry, Mr. Case. Your sister is dead.
She was murdered."

Silence.

"Did you hear what I told you, Mr. Case?"

Nothing.

"I must ask you to come back to Batavia, sir, to
identify your sister's body."

"Murdered? My sister wasn't murdered. She
lives alone. She's always lived alone. She can't
help it. People upset her. *Things* upset her. No
one murders a creature like her. Who would
want to murder her? You're mistaken. You're
simply mistaken. Murder happens to people who
are . . . obtrusive. She isn't. This person, this
body you've found; how was it murdered, Mr.
Kenner?"

"I can understand your reluctance, sir—")

It was the injustice of it, after all. Like killing a
child, like putting a knife into a child again and
again and again.

It is the very minute of Anne's murder and she
knows that her killer stands not far away and that
she cannot escape him. She has tried escaping him
before. When his intention was not to murder her
but to overpower her, to rape her.

"Hello, Anne," he says now. "I think you were
expecting me."

She says nothing. She will not acknowledge him.
She will not give him that satisfaction.

She hears the closet door slam against the wall.
She flinches. She does not turn.

Moments pass.

She stares hard at the dying leaf of the Dracena,

at the pathways of the veins; she sees that they change, from green to red to brown.

She knows this man wants her death. He's told her so. ("You can't help it, Anne, my love. I'm going to murder you someday. I *need* it!")

He says now, "I have a knife, Anne."

She sees the dying leaf of the Dracena very clearly. She puts her hand on a small, white ceramic watering can near the Dracena. She sighs. Both she and the plant are going to die, she knows. She whispers, "Let me . . ." but does not finish the sentence—*Let me water my plant.* She feels that it's a ludicrous thing to say, now, and she does not want to appear ludicrous in front of this man.

"Let you *what*, my love? Let you live?"

She says nothing. She realizes that she's shivering from fear.

He says, "You're toying with me, Anne."

Her eyes water. She wants to plead with him, but she can't. It will do no good, she realizes.

He growls, "Don't toy with me, Anne!"

What can she do? She turns her back completely to him. She makes an offering of herself. Then, desperately, though for only a moment, she wants a field to run in, open sky. It's a memory from childhood. She understands this. She pities herself for it.

She knows that her death is at hand.

"And what if I told you that I loved you, Anne?"

She smiles a little. She thinks, *Of course you don't. How could you love anyone?* Then, all at once, she feels the life, like wakefulness, slipping quickly from her. She gasps. It does no good. This surprises her, frightens her; all her life her breathing has worked.

But it doesn't work now.

Her gasp is no more than a sound.

The air stops at the back of her throat, then the Dracena's dying leaf sweeps past her and the dark hardwood floor comes up.

She's in a wide tunnel.

A bright and friendly light shines at its mouth.

She moves happily toward the light.

FOUR

David threw his blanket and sheet off, swung his feet to the floor, stood.

And grew suddenly dizzy.

He crumbled, caught himself with his hands, so he was on all fours on the gray linoleum. "Damn!" he whispered. He should have realized. He'd been in bed for—what?—five days? Longer? Of course he was going to be weak. He had to give himself time.

He sat back on his haunches, so his long arms hung limply at his sides. He realized that he could not stand. An edge of dizziness floated in his head like water, and it started a hard pellet of nausea in his stomach. He leaned forward again, arms crossed at his stomach, eyes closed. The nausea dissipated, though not completely.

He took a long, deep breath and rocked gently on his haunches. How very connected to this life he was—to his bone and flesh and muscle. His stomach fought him, his head fought him. It was not the way of things in the whole of the universe, he knew. There were places where gravity seemed to work in reverse, and where muscle and bone, foot and hand might easily be creations of the soul and of memory.

He stopped rocking. The nausea was returning, it grew in his stomach like an egg.

He rocked.

The nausea retreated.

Eventually, he felt that he could stand. He pushed himself slowly to his feet and stood very unsteadily for a few seconds. Then, all at once, he found himself sitting on the bed, his heart pumping hard and fast, his head lowered.

He asked himself, *Why do I want to go back? For Anne?* He could not answer it concretely. He thought that of course it was for Anne. To find out why she had been the victim of such obscenity. He needed to know the answer to that question as much as he had needed anything in his life—as much as he had needed air on that hot afternoon five years ago, when the lake had closed around him and tried to suck the life from his body.

But—it was obvious—if he went back, he might not return.

Was that all right? Did that agree with him? Did it soothe him?

He didn't want to think so. He wanted to believe that he wanted one adventure—this life—done before he launched himself into another—the next.

He stood. Quickly, he realized that his legs and head and stomach were going to go along with his idea of leaving the hospital.

In one of the other cities on the Other Side, a man sat eating a green salad in his small, well-lighted apartment. The salad was without dressing, but the man had always preferred it plain and he ate it hungrily.

He was alone in the apartment. The walls were light blue, the ceiling white plaster, the floors bare wood. The man had lived in the apartment for a very long time.

He wore a gray sportscoat and tattered brown pants. He was shoeless. His hands were long and thin and he kept them scrupulously clean. He sported a three-day growth of beard, however, and had been giving thought to letting the beard mature, though it was not what concerned him now.

As he ate, he thought about the names that he'd been recording in his notebook. And he thought about the dreams.

The names came to him from many sources. He was a man who was well liked and much spoken to, and there were many people who knew what he was doing in the apartment. So they shared the names with him (though they didn't use the word *names*; the names were *words*, primarily, though some people called them *symbols*, and others called them *manifestations*). They shared their dreams, too. Like people everywhere, they were interested in knowing themselves better, and they supposed (as the man had suggested) that the names and the dreams were reflective of their inner selves, not merely—as so many believed— reflective of "those on the horizon," which, the man thought, was simply so much superstition, on a par with the widely held belief that there were lives *after* this life. He believed otherwise. He believed that there had been a previous life.

He finished his salad and took his wooden bowl to the sink to wash it. He turned on the faucet, waited a moment while the pipes in the old building clanged and cursed, and at last a spurt of water belched out, hit the bowl and splashed onto his pants. He backed up, though it was too late. He looked down at himself. *Well, I can't go outside like this,* he thought. *It looks like I've peed my pants.*

He also had many books in his library. Those that weren't self-written were donations from friends. He had pored over these books many times, always struck by the similarity between what they recorded and what people had shared verbally with him about their dreams. "But these are not dreams," he had decided, meaning— though he had could not have verbalized it—*these are not fictions.*

He changed his pants and left the room. The stairs to the ground level were long and poorly lit and they moaned ominously. (There were many rooms and apartments in the building but most were uninhabited; most of those that were inhabited were underground. Many people preferred such apartments, though he couldn't imagine why. "I feel more at home underground," these people said.)

When he reached the bottom floor, he went out, onto the street.

It was full of people. Some walked quickly in the bright, early morning light, and he recognized them because they were always the same people. They moved with their heads down and their arms close to their sides, their eyes apparently unmoving. Once, he had asked one of them, "Where are you going this way?" (meaning so quickly and with so little attention to the surroundings; it was, as far as the man was concerned, a very strange way to move about in this beautiful place). That person had stopped suddenly and had given the man a quick and startled look. "I'm going to the countryside. Picnic. Hike," he said, and then had continued walking.

The man knew what picnics and hikes were. He'd been on many picnics and had taken many hikes. But the point was that the countryside would always be there and rushing to it with one's head down neglected the beauty of the city.

Another person had said, "But there is no time." It was a very odd thing to say. What was *time*?

He thought now, as he walked, of the book he had read the previous evening. The book had been given to him by a woman who lived in his building. It spoke of many things which other people had spoken of; but it also spoke of something new. *Famlees.* And, in the same sentence, it referred to *mutherfahthr, sons and dawters.* This, in itself, was not wonderfully new. Several of the other books had spoken of *phauthors* or *fathrs,* or *fahthers,* and of *mawthers* (*mothers, muthars*) which he felt confident were the same as *mutherfahthr.* (They also spoke of *mahmahs* and *dadees,* though he had guessed that there was no connection.) But the book took all the others a giant step further. It linked *mutherfahthr, sons and dawters* under the collective word *famlee.*

"Theze r famlees," the book read. "And tha r guod comfertibel, distent." He knew what the woman meant at once, because as soon as he'd read the words his skin tingled a little and he felt warm. And the word that came from him often came from him then: "Shannon." And like all the other times the word had come from him, it carried with it a feeling of contentment and peace. But there was something else, too. Something that had never come to him before when he had mouthed the word—the mental image of a woman with red hair, large eyes, straight nose, lips slightly parted. This face lingered in his head for a long while, and then very slowly dissipated, like a morning mist.

It occurred to him then that the word *Shannon* had something to do with that woman. Perhaps it described her, somehow—had to do with her total self. She was *Shannon* which meant that she had red hair, large eyes, et cetera. Perhaps it meant that she brought him, particularly, the kind of warm and tingly feeling that he first felt the night before, when he had come across the word *famlee*. He dwelt on these ideas as he walked.

He turned a corner and saw one of the faceless, clearly a child, at the opposite end of the avenue. He thought that the child had come out of a house that many of the newly arrived were seen to come out of (a large house with open doorways and windows; a house that no one used precisely because it was one of the houses that the newly arrived—those who were not faceless—came from) and the man's thoughts turned abruptly from *Shannon* to this child.

He often encountered the faceless when he walked the city's streets, and, like the people around him, he avoided them. Now he thought better of it. This one had such an air of helplessness about him. And fear, too. It was obvious in the way he held his arms outstretched, in the way he walked, as if every footfall held the promise of pain.

It was clear that the child was in a place with which he was unfamiliar, a place that frightened him. Just like one of the newly-born. But the newly-born very quickly overcame their fear. After a few moments, they became ecstatic, as if they had been away for a long time and now were home. The faceless, like this child, came and went as if they walked about in darkness, in a land of sorrow.

And, usually, they were quickly gone. They came and went like dreams. Very rarely, they stayed.

The child called out, "Mama, mama." Fear lay over him like sweat. "Mama, where are you? I can't see you!"

The man looked on wonderingly. He stepped forward, caught the child's hand. The child gasped. The man peered hard into the darkness that was the child's face. He saw all but nothing. Beneath the darkness there was a face constricted in panic; it was like seeing a face through dark ice. The man held the boy's hand tightly.

"What do you *want*?" the man said. "What is *Mama*?" He had no pity for the boy; he had no reason for pitying any creature here, so his tone was flat and apparently stern.

The boy was dressed in black swimming trunks. The man had no idea what swimming trunks were. The boy was wet; his blond hair, which outlined the darkness that was his face, clung to the sides of his head. He shivered.

The man said again, "What is *Mama*?"

The boy said, "Mama?" It was clear that he was weeping. The man knew about weeping. He had heard others weep, especially while they slept. And he had been told that he wept, as well. And laughed, too. Though he also laughed when he was awake. He did not weep when he was awake.

He said, "Why do you do that?"—meaning, *Why do you weep?* He thought that if the boy could answer the question it would lead him to an understanding of his own weeping, and to the weeping of others.

But then the boy was gone, as quickly and as without preamble as so many others. Like a star obliterated by clouds.

The man continued walking at once. There would be other faceless ones, he knew, and he would learn from them.

* * *

What David remembered most vividly about
Anne was the aura of aloneness that surrounded
her. It was not what he wanted most to remember
about her, not the thing that other people noticed
(mostly because they never got a chance to know
her well enough to see it). Other people thought
of her as "disarmingly intelligent," and "softly
pretty" but with "an edge that makes you realize
she's not someone to be toyed with," and as
"vaguely eccentric, all alone in that huge house,
writing poetry." Who knew her as well as he, after
all? He was her twin. He had known her all her
life and had spent most of those years in awe of
her because she so deftly and gracefully con-
cealed her real self behind a facade of strength
and easy wit and affability.

Who else knew her as well as he? Who knew
that behind her apparent strength and wit and affability, she wanted desperately to be alone?

It was not that she disliked other people. She
thought of herself as "inalterably unlike other
people," and so she never cultivated any close
friendships, except with her brother, because she
was aware that he knew her almost as well as she
knew herself, and because she loved him.

He would like to have been her confidant, someone with whom she could share what he saw as
her almost constant torment. But, in the classic
sense of the word, she confided in him only rarely.
Instead, he found that *he* confided in *her*, that her
vulnerability, her aloneness, her very *illness* gave
her a perspective on being alive that he could not
share. Nearly all possibilities were open to him.
He could go anywhere, do practically anything.
She could not. She was confined, by her illness, to
familiar surroundings, and if she wanted to ven-

ture beyond them she had to do it in her imagination, and in her dreams. This, she had told him, gave her a real appreciation for what others, David included, seemed to take for granted—the freedom to move beyond the limits of the four walls they called home.

FIVE

Christian Grieg put the phone down and stared blankly at Karen Duffy.

"What is it?" she asked.

A smile flickered across his lips, then was gone. Karen barely noticed it. He said, "David's left the hospital."

"What do you mean, 'left the hospital'?"

"I mean he walked out. He just walked out. Someone wasn't doing their job, someone wasn't *watching* him, and he just walked out."

"But . . . he wasn't supposed to do that, was he?"

"Of course he wasn't," Christian snapped. "He was under observation, for Christ's sake!"

"Don't snap at me, Christian." Her voice was firm.

"Yes," he said noncommittally. "I'm sorry."

"Do they know where he went?"

"Apparently not. He's simply not there. He simply *walked out*."

They had been about to share a meal when he made his call to the hospital, at her insistence. The small table was set; the food waited to be served. But now Christian said, "We have to go."

"Where?" Karen asked.

"To find him."

"Do you think we could eat first?"

"No. There's no time. Maybe we'll catch a bite at some . . . at one of those fast food restaurants."

Karen was confused by Christian's almost desperate enthusiasm to go in search of David. She wanted to get at the root of it, so she chose to delay him, which, she thought, would ultimately give her answers faster than direct questions would.

"It won't take but a half hour to eat." she told him.

He gave her a disbelieving smile. "My friend is in trouble—"

"We have no proof of it," she cut in. She stood, walked past him into his kitchen, collected a bowl of vegetables and a bowl of pasta and carried them to the table. She looked at him. She said, "You can bring the wine in. And the sauce."

He watched her silently, his mouth agape.

She pressed, "Did you hear me, Christian?"

"At the moment, food is unimportant," he told her, but his voice was weak and unconvincing. After a second, he added, his voice a little stronger, "Don't do this, Karen."

"Do what?"

"I have to go. I have to find David. I have to know . . ." He stopped.

"Yes?"

"Are you coming with me?"

"What do you have to know, Christian?"

He ignored her question. "Are you coming? I'm not going to eat. I'm going to look for David."

"Dammit, what do you have to *know*, Christian?"

But he didn't answer, and within seconds he was out the door.

Getting into Laude Pharmaceuticals was easy enough. David still had his ID card, and he knew the security guards.

The guard who let him in was a chubby, middle-aged man named Walt.

"I heard you were sick, Mr. Case," Walt said, apparently surprised to see David so late at night. Walt checked his watch; it read 12:15. "Going to be working late?"

David nodded and held out his ID card. Walt said it wasn't necessary, then looked at it just the same because David's face was thinner than he remembered and it had the beginnings of a beard. "Thanks," Walt said, handing it back. Then, after a short look into David's eyes, he said, "Are you sure you're all right, Mr. Case? You don't look very good."

"Yes," David said, "I'm okay. It's nothing. Thanks for your concern."

"Yes sir," Walt said, and opened the door.

Then David was walking through the maze of corridors—lit dimly now—which led to his laboratory. And as he walked he thought of Anne, saw her face in his mind's eye; saw it as if it were the face of a child. It was the way he had always thought of her, he realized. She was his twin, just as old as he was, but, in some ways, he thought of her as a child, especially in the past few years. Perhaps because of her vulnerability and her sensitivity. Her handicap. Her aloneness.

And as he turned and started down the final corridor to his laboratory, he wondered if that hand-

icap had stayed with her; if, now—under some
vast, bright, and unknown sky—she was on the
verge of panic, desperately wanted walls around
her, a floor beneath her, a roof overhead.

He closed his eyes. God, he prayed that it wasn't
true. Why should such torture follow the incredible obscenity of her rape and murder? Wasn't it
obvious that death was the end of such imperfec-
tion? Weren't the blind suddenly sighted, the deaf
able to hear even the whisper of small insects;
weren't the paraplegic as swift and surefooted as
any earthbound creature? But those were very different kinds of handicaps. They were centered in
the blood and bone and nerves. Anne's handicap
went much deeper. It lived in the deepest recesses
of her mind. She had never *known* why she was
the way she was. No one had. But she'd suffered
with it for half a lifetime.

And there was no guarantee now that she was
not still suffering.

David stopped walking suddenly. He shook his
head. "Good Lord," he whispered. It wasn't possible. How could she possibly have carried her illness with her into death? It was insanity even to
consider it.

But he had to consider it.

Because, in life, *she* had considered it.

("David, I think that this . . . thing, this sickness
is part of *me*, part of my *soul*. I can *feel* it. It's the
way I've always been. I think that I will never be
without it."

"I don't know what you're talking about, Annie.
Really, I don't."

"Someday you will, David.")

And what if she were right? What if—how old
had she been?—her fifteen- or sixteen-year-old
mind, a mind which had always been so much

keener than his, so much more in tune with the world around it (which was, after all, its undoing), had whispered to her an awful and undeniable truth: that her sickness would follow her through eternity.

If that were so, then the place where she dwelt now had truly to be hell.

David could not deny that the possibility was very real; as hard as he tried, he could not rationalize it away. It stayed. It mocked him. It screamed that as much as he wanted to believe that death had brought peace to his sister at last, he could easily be wrong.

In his office, he located the A2d-40 he needed and within minutes had left the building and was driving to his cottage on Oneida Lake.

It is ten years later. Maude is standing quietly just inside the doorway to the third floor ballroom. She's wondering if Anne ever came to this room—because she knows that Anne lived alone; she thinks that a woman living alone would have no reason to come up here—and she's trying to sense Anne's spirit in this huge space, trying to catch sight of it as—Maude supposes—it moves sullenly from place to place.

This is a bright, early summer morning, and shafts of yellow sunlight filter in through the tall windows. There's a lot of fine dust in the air. Maude notes it. She remembers reading that most house dust is made up of bits of human skin.

The dust diffuses the sunlight.

She fancies, then, that she sees something dark and (she strains to see and understand) . . . tense moving in the far half of the empty room, through the diffuse sunlight. She smiles uneasily. Dark and *tense*? No. Dark and *graceful*. That would be Anne. That would be the spirit of Anne Case.

But then the thing is gone suddenly and she stops smiling. "Anne?" she whispers. "Are you still here, Anne?" There is no sound. The room is quiet and empty and the sunlight is diffuse and nothing moves.

When she leaves the room a quarter of an hour later, she locks the door behind her. She's not sure why. She believes that Anne's spirit is gentle and nonaggressive. She believes that she would welcome it, speak with it, if it showed itself. But she's not sure what, exactly, she saw in the third floor ballroom. Something tall, stocky, mannish, her memory tells her, but she rejects that image out of hand. She does not want a spirit that is tall, stocky, and mannish moving about in her house. That would be the stuff that nightmares are made of. Better a lithe and gentle spirit. The spirit of Anne Case.

"I saw her today," she tells her husband later.

"Who? Our spook?" he says.

"Please don't refer to her that way. It's . . . disrespectful."

Peter chuckles a bit; then, upon a scornful look from Maude, says, "I didn't mean to be disrespectful. 'Spook' is a very acceptable word."

"No. Not to me. It's . . . ungentle, uncaring. Doesn't it . . . move you, Peter, that some poor woman was *murdered* here? Think of the agony she must have suffered."

"I would say that any murder victim probably feels agony, Maude."

"Yes, but not just *any* murder victim's spirit walks about in *our* house."

There's silence for a moment. Then Peter says, "You're really quite sure of that, aren't you?"

"Yes."

"That simple?"

"For God's sake, Peter, I've *seen* her."

"Have you? I mean, have you *really*? Enough that if you were to see her photograph you could say, 'Yes, the spook I saw in my house is this woman'?"

Silence.

"Maude?" Peter coaxes.

"I've seen her photograph. I went to the newspaper and looked in their morgue—that's what they call their library of old newspapers, you know. A morgue. Makes me shudder. And, yes, the spirit I've seen here is definitely Anne. I have no doubt of it."

"Same eyes? Same nose, same mouth? Everything matches?"

"Oh, dammit, Peter! Not everything in life can be . . . quantified."

"Quantified?"

"You know what I mean. Not everything is black or white, hot or cold, up or down." She pauses. "No, if I have to be entirely truthful, I have *not* seen the woman in the photograph. There, do you feel better? Does that make you feel superior, Peter?"

"No reason to get angry." He's concerned. She's making much more of the whole thing than he thinks is healthy. "I just can't say that I'm as . . . caught up in this—"

"But I *know* it's Anne as surely as I know anything. Didn't I tell you I saw her today? Didn't I tell you that?"

"What exactly *did* you see?"

"Her, dammit! *Anne Case!* Upstairs, in that big room on the third floor. She was there, and I saw her." A quick pause, then Maude hurries on, "Not her *face*, if that's what you're wondering, not her eyes, or her mouth. I don't need to see any of that, Peter, because I *sensed* her."

"Anne Case?" Peter says resignedly.

"Yes. Anne Case." The image of the tall, stocky, mannish figure in the third floor ballroom has all but receded into her subconscious. She recalls it only briefly, pushes it back. "Anne Case," she says again, with feeling.

David sat rigidly on the edge of his bed in his cottage on Oneida Lake. He was apprehensive. A strange sense of elation filled him and it made him fearful, uncertain: How well did he know himself, after all? This well? He focused on the four blue capsules—A2d-40—in his open right hand. Did he know himself well enough to trust that he was going back for all the right reasons?

To find Anne?

To confront her killer? (If Brian Fisher had indeed been her killer; David wasn't sure, and he didn't know why he wasn't sure.)

To assure himself that death had brought peace to her, at last?

Or was he going back because something very deep inside him intended to stay? Because something inside him needed the peace that that place seemed to offer?

If he had asked himself the same questions three weeks earlier—before Anne's death—he thought that his answer would have been a quick laugh.

His gaze drifted slightly. It took in his fingers, which were long and pale; the third finger curved slightly outward, toward the little finger. An accident thirty years before had caused that curvature. Occasionally the finger ached dully, as if there were something growing inside it. He had wondered often if, as he aged, the finger would give him more constant pain. He thought now, *The strange links we have with our past and our future.*

And then he raised his hand and put first one, then another of the blue capsules of A2d-40 into his mouth. There was a tall glass half-filled with water on a table next to the bed. He drank all the water.

Within a minute, he felt groggy.

Shortly after that, he was asleep.

SIX

Anne Case's killer often remembered the moment of her death. And when he did, it was with great regret, because her death had happened with such numbing swiftness.

He had not wanted it to be so quick. It had been like turning out a light. He wanted to enjoy her, her agony and her confusion. He had been entitled—*she* had entitled him. But, as was often said of orgasm, the whole thing had been an anticlimax.

It could not be helped, though. It had been the luck of the draw, the twist of fate—it had happened the way it had happened and nothing would ever change it.

He could take what pleasure he could from what *had* happened. But what had happened was so very unimpressive—life metamorphosing into death over the period of a moment or two. No confusion. No agony.

In his mental replaying of these moments, he sometimes had Anne Case turn and face him and he imagined that her face was twisted with fear. But that was ultimately unsatisfying because he knew that it was a fiction. It was more satisfying to keep her mentally turned away and imagine that her face, hidden from him, had been twisted by fear. Logically, it could have been no other way. If he had been in her shoes, fear would have paralyzed him. He would have had no choice but to surrender to whatever the moment had in store.

But he had *known* her and he knew now that fear simply could not have entangled her the way he had so desperately wanted it to. Fear already wrapped her up and entangled her from within, and had for decades. How could he hope to bring it to her from without? He had been aware of that, he realized now, even as he had watched from inside her closet as she tended to her damned plant.

He had even known it when he had raped her and she had simply *watched* him do it. Christ, he had nearly killed her then. How could she have simply *watched* him? It was unnatural!

But it was too bad that she was dead. She had been a good plaything. She had brought him pleasure. She'd bouyed him up and had shown him what a class act he was, had confirmed it for him. Certainly she was a discriminating woman. It was obvious even in the way she furnished her house— with sturdy utilitarian pieces.

She was no one's fool.

But neither was he. *She* had proven it. She had not made a fool of him.

Except, perhaps, in the way she had died.

But it had not been her choice. It had been the

luck of the knife. The slant of her back and the luck of the knife. She was too thin, the knife a centimeter too long. Perhaps if she had not been bending over. Perhaps in bending over she had brought her heart closer to the point of the knife. It was reasonable.

And he was a reasonable man.

David, lying on his back, hands at his sides, his head against the trunk of a fallen tree, was aware that he was naked. It embarrassed him. It reminded him strongly of dreams of being naked; of his vast humiliation, in those dreams, at his own nakedness. But no one but he had ever cared about it in his dreams, and there was no one to care about it here.

He remembered that he had not been naked when he had come here before. This was new. This was different. And he didn't know what to make of it. His body displeased him, for one thing. It was out of shape, not hairy enough—considering that male bodies should always be hairy around the chest, at least—and his genitals were too obvious against his pale thighs; they were genitals which could not be taken for granted, even amidst general nakedness.

It occurred to him that his nakedness was a symbol—all too real—of his death.

That was a possibility he could not dismiss. Perhaps he really was dead, here, amongst the trees, and the dust hanging in the air, and the cold light.

He wanted clothes, suddenly. He was cold, and naked, and he wanted clothes.

The tree against which his head rested was clearly long dead because moss covered it and he could feel, beneath his skull, that it was fleshy, soft.

He scrambled to his feet, aware of the insects that lived in such trees, that fed on such decay. He stared at the trunk of the tree; he saw that there *were* insects on it—elongated, gunmetal blue insects which moved fluidly about on the tree trunk, some carrying bits of the rust-red meat of the tree with them.

He swiped at his hair, convinced that some of these insects were moving about in it. But his hand passed over nothing but his hair and his skull, so he was able to calm himself.

He dwelt on his nakedness again. Now he found it vaguely stimulating—as it always had been in his dreams—and he listened closely for voices from within the forest to tell him that he was on the verge of being found.

It came to him suddenly that he did not remember going through a tunnel toward the light. It was what had happened before, both a week ago, and, as well, five years ago, when he had nearly drowned. But he *must* have gone through the tunnel. It was the way *into* this place, after all; it was the entrance, the door. He could not have gotten here otherwise. But he didn't remember it. Clearly, he had simply forgotten.

But he had forgotten nothing else.

Again he focused on his nakedness. He looked down at himself and thought that he was exposed, vulnerable. It did not stimulate him. He thought of bees and remembered that they were drawn to the smell of sweat. He thought that if there were bees here they would be drawn to him because, he could see now, he was sweating.

And then he saw that there *were* bees. Big fat honeybees that drifted from here to there—from flower to flower; one from a spray of tiny purple flowers near the trunk of the dead tree to what looked like dandelions close by, and then to the clover, which was in abundance. Others flew slowly, their wings straining against the load of pollen they carried. There were a dozen bees, David thought. Two dozen. And he was afraid for himself because of his nakedness.

Because bees were drawn to sweat and he was sweating.

It made him afraid.

He clutched at himself and walked stiffly from the place.

He found a path through the forest and he took it; but there were hundreds of bees on it, and the light was very cold; the dust choked him.

And a ghost of the earth existed here.

At the horizon, there was a line of squat, gaily painted cottages a half mile across the lake.

The lake.

It was as overpowering as fog. As near as fog. It misted his fingers. He was walking in it.

Still, there were the bees. Hundreds of bees.

He clutched at himself. He cried out, "Where am I?" He didn't know. "Where in hell *am* I?"

This was not the place he had wanted to come to.

This was too familiar and too strange. This had the ghost of the earth on it.

It had the lake on it.

"Where *am* I?" he cried.

Then he thought he knew where he was. And he realized that he had gone nowhere, that he wasn't naked, that the ghost of the earth which shimmered around him *was* the earth.

Because he could smell it now.

He could smell the lake that he stood in up to midthigh.

He looked down at himself. He saw that he

was wearing his gray pants and green shirt and, off-angle through the clear water, his penny loafers.

It was dusk. The mosquitoes had gathered above the water and they were satisfying themselves on him.

He closed his eyes, put his hands over them, whispered, "I've gone nowhere." It made him happy. It made him unhappy.

It made him desperate to try again.

He trudged to shore and then—past the remains of a half dozen thin translucent fish—to his small green cottage.

He did not get through the side doorway. He collapsed on the narrow porch.

He saw the tunnel opening. It floated tiny and white in a field of darkness, like a small, dying sun. He reached for it. The image of his hand covered it and it was gone. But then he took his hand away and it reappeared.

He moved toward it as if he were caught in a vortex. It tugged relentlessly at him and made him afraid.

Shapes pushed up toward him from the darkness. He thought they were hands but they were the color and form of darkness, and their fingers were like fingers of dark earth.

And he knew that they *were* the hands of the earth trying to draw him back.

But the tunnel opening widened inexorably, without the passage of time—it was *this* wide, it was *this* wide, it was *this* wide.

As wide as the moon hanging in the darkness.

As wide as the edges of his vision.

And it was a fragile and pale blue, like the blue that follows the red of sunset.

It engulfed him, and the darkness was no more. He was engulfed. Swallowed. Within.

He was underwater and being tugged inexorably and endlessly toward the sun.

He was being pulled by daylight from the depths of a dream.

Fred Collins said to Leo Kenner, "I just can't believe that there's nothing to implicate him." He was talking about Brian Fisher. He had the file on Anne Case opened in front of him. There was also a small pile of personal effects—a few letters, her purse, a telephone number–address book—at the front of his desk, near where it touched Leo Kenner's desk.

Leo Kenner nodded. "It happens," he said. "Sometimes people just don't put things down in writing."

"But *he* would have, Leo. And *she* would have, too."

"Yes." Leo sighed. "I'm aware of that." He shrugged. "But we can't expect that everything will be tied up neatly."

"Why not?" Collins asked. "Given the circumstances, why not? What have we got here? I mean *look* at it: We've got an agoraphobic who spends virtually all of her time inside her house. We know from talking to her brother that she was fond of writing poetry, which *assumes* that she also liked to write letters, and except for the agoraphobia, her boyfriend—Brian Fisher—is cut from the same mold. And we find *his* letters and *his* poetry, but we find nothing in *her* house."

"She might have kept those things elsewhere," Leo suggested; then, realizing it was a lame remark, added, "It's possible."

"No, it isn't," Collins protested. "If she spent all of her time inside her house, Leo—"

"*Most* of her time."

"If she spent all the time that *matters* inside her house, then *that* is where she would keep her letters and her poetry. But what do we have?" He picked up the letters on his desk. "A few notes to her brother about his birthday and his new job. It makes no damned sense, Leo."

"So search her place again," Leo said.

Collins shook his head. "I don't want to do that. It's been searched . . . thoroughly. I don't want to go inside it again."

Leo looked confusedly at him. "Something's bothering you, Fred. Why don't you share it with me."

Again Collins shook his head. "I think . . . I merely think that it would waste our time to go through Anne's house again. *I've* been through it. *Forensics* has been through it. There's *nothing* there—nothing that pertains, anyway—that we're not aware of."

Kenner's brow furrowed. "Did you know her, Fred?"

"Sorry?"

"You referred to her as 'Anne.' "

"Did I?" He smiled a little, then caught himself. "I wasn't . . . aware of it. I'm sorry. I guess I've been thinking about her . . . about this investigation, quite a bit. And when you do that, it . . . makes you believe, after a while, that you *know* a person. A victim. I'm sure I've done the same sort of thing before."

Kenner paused. "If you have, I don't remember it."

"Uh-huh. Well *I'm* sure I have." He smiled quickly, as if to dismiss the subject. "Yes," he went on, "I'll take another look. Tomorrow. Maybe tonight."

"Tomorrow's Sunday."

"It's okay. I don't mind. Sunday's good. I wasn't going to be doing anything else, anyway."

It's three weeks before her murder, and Anne is talking with David in the cavernous third floor ballroom in her big house. She nods at a tall, broad-leafed plant, a Dracena, in the far corner of the room. "It's dying. There's nothing I can do about it," she says.

"Water it," David says.

She shakes her head very seriously. It's not an emotional thing, the death of her plant, and that is clear to David.

"I've done that," she tells him. "It does no good. It's dying for some other reason. Old age, probably."

"I didn't know plants died of old age."

She smiles at him as if he has told her a joke, although his remark was serious. "Yes. Plants aren't immortal."

They are seated together on a big couch that rarely gets used because she and her brother are the only ones who come to this room. Her moods usually prevent her from coming to the room alone because it's so big, and although there are heavy curtains on the bay window, Oriental rugs scattered around the floor, and several heavy, upholstered pieces of furniture in the room, voices echo in it, reminding her of its bigness. But she does not mind coming here with her brother. It's almost, she's told him, like going for a walk in the countryside, which she hasn't done for decades.

He has not seen her for some time because of the pressures of his job. He's missed her. She's intelligent and philosophical; all their lives they have enjoyed each others' company. But he's having trouble breaking through the barrier that time apart has set up between them. He asks her, "What have you been up to, Annie?"

She smiles. "You haven't called me that in a very long time." She pauses, though not long enough to give him a chance to answer. "I've been very good. I'm happy, David. I have a lover."

He doesn't know how to respond to this. He's aware that he's suddenly staring at her dumbly and he's sure that some inappropriate look of shock or surprise is transforming his features. He knows that she requires comment, but he can think of nothing. He says lamely, "Yes?"

"Yes. He's a nice boy," she says, and again she shakes her head and smiles, but self-consciously, now. "He's not a boy, David. He *looks* like a boy, I think. Sometimes, anyway. He looks vulnerable, at least." Again she shakes her head, then looks down at her hands folded in her lap. "I'm handling this very, very poorly, aren't I? I knew that my ... revelation would be important. To you."

And it was, of course. She had rarely talked with him about the men in her life before, although there had been several, he knew. Most recently, a man with whom she had had a very brief but apparently very volatile relationship, a man she now refused to talk about, a man whom David had never met. The men in her life were just about the only things she didn't talk to him about; where to live, how to spend her money, how best to deal with her illness, how to deal with friends and relatives who thought they knew best what she should do with her life—given the restrictions imposed by her illness—all these things and more were topics she discussed freely. Her love life had gone almost totally undiscussed.

"What's there to handle poorly, Anne?" David asks. "I'm glad you feel free to talk with me about it." There is an emotion—jealously?—pushing up from deep inside him and he tries to push it back. "What's his name?"

She shakes her head. She doesn't want to tell him the man's name, she says. Maybe after a while.

This makes David uncomfortable. She feels free to discuss the *fact* of the man with him, but not something so mundane as his name. Clearly she is holding something back. "What's in a name?" he asks, and smiles.

"Lots," she answers.

"Is it someone I know?"

She shakes her head. He's not sure if she's saying no, he's not someone David knows, or no, she doesn't want to discuss it.

David says, "It's not the man you were involved with six months ago, is it?"

Suddenly, Anne looks as if she's in pain. "No," she whispers. "God, no!"

"Sorry," David says, then, smiling: "Can you describe him, Anne? That way I'll at least have a mental picture of this man who has designs on my twin sister." Yes, he realizes, it *is* jealousy he feels; and it is one of the reasons he's been only too happy, in the past, not to discuss with her any of the other men in her life.

"Describe him?" She grins slyly, as if to tell him she knows he's playing a game with her, but that she'll play along. "Yes, I can describe him. With or without his clothes, David?"

He smiles quickly at this, but too broadly, and for too long. "Well, yes," he begins, and forces his smile down so that it is merely a grin. "With his clothes, I think. I've seen naked men, Anne."

"Have it your way." She acts disappointed. "He's . . . forgettable."

"Ha. This sounds like the real thing, Annie."

"Maybe it is, David." She pauses. "I feel happy when I'm with him. I think that's important."

David nods. "If you're happy, then so am I," he says and, he realizes with surprise, it's true.

She smiles. "You'll meet him tonight, David. I'm having both of you over for dinner."

SEVEN

Karen Duffy could not believe that Christian had simply left the house. When would he return? *Would* he return? But that was silly. Of course he would. Why would she even ask the question?

She didn't know what to do. She was worried about him, worried about his irrational behavior in the past few days—in reality, ever since David's apparent suicide attempt. But she did not like being in his house. In point of fact, she did not like being with him anymore. She did it only out of respect for the idea of love that had developed between them.

Perhaps that's all it was. An idea. Something they had cultivated because it was something that was easy to cultivate.

She had known him for several years. Why now, only in the past few weeks, had she "discovered" that she loved him? Perhaps something inside her

was playing a kind of easy and convenient game,
both with her and with him—with both of them.

But where was he now? And why had he so desperately needed to go after David?

"We must ask important questions," the tall,
apparently middle-aged woman exhorted the
crowd before her. Her long dark hair, touched by
gray at the temples, shown in the light. Her blue
eyes were wide with excitement and wonder. "We
must ask about *bone structure, tea leaves, disco,
whole life, mini-buses, catsup, napkin rings, toilet
articles, pinkie rings, Meerschaums, etiquette,
rose, talking boards, hauntings, love signs.* All of
these have come to me in dreams. The dreams can
tell us much, if only we know how to interpret
them."

An apparently young man in the crowd called
out, "But these dreams don't *mean* anything.
They're just . . . images in the head. And these
words, which we've all heard, I think, are only
whispers in the dark." There was no sarcasm or
chastisement in his tone. He was making a simple
statement of fact, as he saw it.

The woman said, shaking her head, "No. I think
they're as important as . . ." She paused, then
continued, "Somehow, I believe that they're as important as the darkness that interrupts the day."

A few in the crowd, shaking their heads in be-
wilderment, moved off toward the lush green forest nearby. There had always been people who
talked the way this woman was talking, and there
always would be. It did not effect the way things
were. Things were as they were for reasons that
no once could understand. The darkness interrupted the day for its own reasons. Words came
to them all in dreams for unfathomable reasons
(reasons, perhaps, that only the Creator could un-

derstand). Talking about it was a futile gesture. Better to keep moving.

"I've heard these words in dreams," the woman reiterated, as if to underscore their importance. But it was a pronouncement that others had made. *"I have heard these words in dreams*—words like *Mousketeer*, and *Yankee Doodle Dandy*, and *New Deal, laissez-faire, steam calliope."* Nothing had ever been found in the words, or in the dreams that spawned them, that bore significance, although there had always been those, like this woman, who argued that their significance lay in what was to come, in the existence that followed this existence.

So some who were listening wandered off into the forest nearby, because they had heard many others make pronouncements such as she was making.

David, who was standing just inside the perimeter of the forest, could not hear her. He heard only a high-pitched humming sound, like a distant hive of bees.

But he could see the woman clearly. She was on a small rise; he could see the crowd around her, and those that had turned away and were walking toward him, toward the forest.

The people in the crowd and the people walking toward him were dressed in many ways—some in hoopskirts, some in jeans and T-shirts, some in garish bermuda shorts, a few in suits. And their faces were masked in shadow. He saw only the suggestion of faces beneath, as if he were looking at these faces through dark water.

The day was bright and cloudless.

There was a frenzy of light at the horizon, as if the sun were shining through thick, moving, and imperfect glass.

Around him, there were the commingled sounds

of animals, though he heard only the high-pitched humming sound he had heard since the tunnel had pulled him here.

And he was very frightened. More frightened, even, than he would have been at the prospect of his own death. Because he was in a place whose sounds he could not hear, and the people in it had faces that he could not see.

And he could not feel the tug of gravity from below.

And the patchwork landscape was the soft landscape of a dream.

And the breezes caressed his face too strongly, as if intending to redo it and make it into someone else's.

And the tall grasses clutched at his bare feet like hands reaching for him from the earth beneath.

And though he asked himself again and again, *Where am I?*, he had no answer.

Fred Collins wondered where he would look first. Because all of the *official* looking had been done, and it had been incredibly thorough. Everything in the house, the house that had kept Anne Case company in the last ten years of her short and painful life, had been catalogued and investigated and compared. Cupboards and drawers had been looked into and then looked into again; even the shelf paper had been taken up. Acoustical ceilings in the kitchen and dining room had been dismantled and then put back together. The five chests of drawers in the house had been stripped of their contents and examined thoroughly. A grandfather clock on the first floor had been denuded of its working parts, and then reassembled; though, after that, it no longer kept time. The rugs had been looked under, and the closets peered into a half dozen times; clothes—blouses, pants, dresses, underwear, bras—had been handled by first one investigator, then another, and yet another. The pocket of a blouse had yielded what looked to be the beginnings of a letter, but there had been no salutation, only the words, in pencil, on a yellow legal pad: *There is a monster in the house. It comes to me at night and mocks me.* The legal pad itself had not been found. The three wastebaskets in the house had been empty.

So, whatever secrets Anne Case had that might have helped in the investigation of her murder were secrets that had not been unearthed in the thorough search of her house.

No letters. No poetry. (Though her brother, David, had said that she wrote poetry; it was possible, Collins thought, that she destroyed whatever she wrote, thinking it unworthy even of saving. The idea seemed farfetched. People who wrote were, he guessed, people who usually saved what they wrote. Wasn't that part and parcel of the process of writing?) And there had been nothing hidden in books, nothing in the attic except the usual attic accumulations of an old house which had supported an old family; accumulations (a dollhouse, a rocking horse, trunks filled with useless clothing, postcards—circa 1940—a clothes tree, a battered oak armoire) which had yielded nothing to the investigation. The house had been clean. Or, as Collins had thought more than once, it had been *cleaned*. That was an idea which was shared not only by Leo Kenner, but by the homicide captain, as well, and by the forensics people who had gone through the house.

The only fingerprints in the house had been Anne's. Partials of another person's fingerprints—found in the third floor ballroom—had been useless.

Investigation of carpet fibers had shown that the only dirt imbedded in the rugs was dirt that had probably come from just outside the house, where Anne kept her garden.

Foodstuffs in the refrigerator and the cupboards—indicative of Anne's vegetarianism—had shown no hint that she had been entertaining someone, or planned to.

The house had been clean. *Cleaned.*

And that was certainly not the act of someone who later confesses, and then commits suicide, Collins told himself. Cleaning the house so very thoroughly was the product of brutal calculation. Brian Fisher had been a man possessed by his passions, a man clearly and deeply in love with Anne Case.

Collins sighed. If it was all true, then so what? Where did it take him? Only here. Back to the house. Back to Anne Case's house.

He closed the door behind him, flicked the light switch. No lights came on. He tried the switch again. "Dammit!" he breathed. He crossed the short hall to the expansive living room and tried the switch there. The crystal ceiling fixture stayed dark. The room held the soft, yellowish glow of late afternoon sunlight filtered through windows in the west wall of the house.

There were several heavy, functional-looking pieces here—a red couch, a blue upholstered wing chair, walnut bookcases brimming with books against one wall. The floor was bare, random-width pine.

Collins stepped into the living room. He hesitated.

He could feel Anne in here. Not her spirit, but the substance of her that she had left behind. It was gentle and probing; and there was humor in it, too. He liked that. He could hear her soft, pleasant laughter ringing through the house.

He said, "Who did you let in to this house, Anne?"

The room darkened slightly as clouds passed in front of the sun. Then it lightened.

He went to the phone on a small dark table next to the couch, dialed Information, got the number of the local electric utility company. He dialed the number.

Five minutes later, he had learned that Anne Case, at 115 Troy Road, had not paid her bill, so the electricity and the gas had been turned off the day before.

He hung up. He could try to get it turned on under a police order. But for now he was content merely to be here, in her house, inhaling the substance and fragrance of her, being *with* her, being a part of her existence, which continued. Of course. Continued in her house; her *things* continued it. And there was nothing metaphysical about that. Nothing mystical. People became their *things*—their homes, their belongings, their clothing, their furniture. Their letters. Their poetry.

"Hello, Anne," he said. It was not the first time he had said hello to her, but it was the first time that he had been so aware of it, and so embarrassed by it, as if someone were watching. He repeated it, as if that would negate his embarrassment, as if the very *fact* of his words would overcome his growing consciousness of them.

"Hello, Anne."

The sound of his voice was lost in the big, darkening room; the heavy furniture soaked it up, the bare floors threw a whisper in echo back to him, as if it were an afterthought.

"Hello, Anne."

"Hello, Anne."

Dammit, who murdered you?

But there was no small answering echo to that question.

"Who murdered you, Anne?" he whispered. He barely heard himself.

"Who in hell murdered you?" he said aloud. The sound of his voice whispering back from the big room unnerved him. He wished suddenly that the lights were working, that there was more than the dying light of late afternoon here.

"Talk to me, Anne," he pleaded.

But he knew that she was beyond that. Only the Anne that existed in his brain talked to him.

EIGHT

David put his hand on the shoulder of a woman with long, black hair. The woman stopped walking and turned her face toward him. He tried hard to peer through the darkness there, around her face. He saw the suggestion of lips, the glimmer of eyes turned questioningly toward him. But perhaps this, he told himself, was only what he thought he *should* see, as if he were looking at a cartoon face that was minus one or more of its parts—the mind fills in the missing parts.

He said, exaggerating the movements of his mouth and speaking loudly—as if the woman were deaf, or did not fully understand his words—"Do you recognize me? Who *am* I? Is there more to this?"

The darkness that was her face tilted slightly, as if in confusion. She said, in a voice that was clear and musical, but oddly tense, "Please, sir, you frighten me."

David shook his head. "I don't understand that." He paused. "I'm . . . lost." He nodded toward the forest behind him. "I came from in there." He shook his head again. "And now I'm out here, but I don't know where here *is*."

He heard laughter. He peered hard at the face of the black-haired woman and saw beneath the darkness that covered it the same full lips and the same eyes he had seen before. She was not laughing and yet he could hear peals of laughter that could be coming from no one else. There was no one else nearby. In the little hollow where the other woman was telling her listeners to "ask important questions," there were many people, but the hollow was far off, and the laughter he heard was practically at his ear.

He asked the black-haired woman, "Is something funny?"

"Please, sir," she repeated, "you frighten me. I can't *see* you."

And as she spoke, the laughter continued. As an overlay to it, he heard, "You cannot stay here." The voice was clearly not hers; it was a voice that was essentially sexless, and it had come from behind him.

He looked back. He saw nothing.

"You'll find out," said the voice. "You'll find out that you can't stay. I'm not joking with you. You'll see. There's pain if you stay. This isn't something you should treat lightly."

David whirled, but there was no one behind him, only the forest, green and lush.

"Who *are* you?" he shouted.

"Get your business done with," said the voice. "You think you've got time to dawdle? You don't. Believe me. I'm not joking here."

"*Who* are you?"

"I would say, 'Who are you?' Do you know? You must know. It's very important that you know. You start losing track of yourself and you'll be lost forever."

Nearby, a rectangle of earth in the dimensions of a man rose and fell very slightly, as if it were breathing. It was covered with pale green grass, and as David watched, the woman he had been talking to walked over the moving spot of earth. It rose through the bottom inch or so of her foot, caressed it a moment, then let it go easily as the woman passed into the forest.

David became aware of his nakedness then, seeing the woman's sandaled foot. *I don't have any clothes on*, he thought.

A grainy numbness—low and insistent—started around his eyes and forehead; he barely noticed it. Oddly, it was almost pleasant.

He thought, *I have pain*. He closed his eyes. He studied the pain, wondered at it.

He heard waves whispering to shore, the distant squawk of gulls, the low, moist sputter of an outboard motor. He opened his eyes. He saw nothing nearby that would cause such sounds. He saw the forest, like a dark green mouth, and turning his head to look in the opposite direction, he saw the woman in the hollow still exhorting her listeners to "ask important questions," and, around the hollow, a checkerboard landscape that reached very, very far in three directions; and beyond that landscape, the deep, cloudless gray-blue sky in turmoil, as if sunlight were trying to break through thick, and imperfect, moving glass.

From his left, he heard, "I want to talk to you." He looked. A man even taller than himself, but very thin, so the bones of his shoulders jutted out from beneath reedy muscles, went on, "Yes, you.

I want to ask you questions." The man was dressed in a gray sportscoat and tattered white pants, and his thick, light brown hair shot out in all directions. But his face, like all the faces here, was a mask of darkness. David could see only the suggestion of a full mouth and broad nose. "Yes, you," the man repeated.

"Who are you?" David asked.

"I don't understand that," the man said peevishly. " 'Who are you?' "

But David didn't realize the man was repeating his question, so he said, "I don't know who I am."

The man sighed. "Can you come with me?"

"To where?"

"To my apartment."

A face appeared in David's memory. It was pale, fine-featured, gray-eyed; and it was surrounded by darkness.

"I want to talk to you," the thin man with the unruly hair went on. "I want to ask you questions. I think you can help me. I think you can help us all."

"I don't know," David said again, his mental eye on the pale and fine-featured face that filled his memory. His pain deepened a little as he looked at it. He winced, though not so much in response to the pain as in response to the possibility that it would continue to increase.

"I want you to come with me," the man said again. "I have things to show you." He paused. "Can you *see* through that; can you *hear*?"

"Through what?" David asked. "Who are you?"

"I don't understand that," the man said. " 'Who are you?' "

"I don't know," David said, again misunderstanding what the man had said. "Dammit, I don't know!"

The man sighed.

The face in David's memory smiled.

"Anne?" David whispered.

"*Anne?*" the man said. "What is that? *Anne.*"

But David's eyes were on the face of his sister, smiling in his memory. The face disappeared. The pain encircling David's head increased. He winced again.

And suddenly he knew where he was and what he was doing. And why.

He looked down at himself. "I don't have any damned clothes on," he whispered.

"But you do," said the man standing with him.

"No, I don't," David said, then continued, as if seeing the man for the first time, "Who are you? Can you help me? Can you tell me where my sister is?"

"Sister? What *is* that? What is *sister*? Tell me about *sister*. Is it connected to *mutherfother*?"

David's gaze went quickly from here to there. It took in the little hollow, the woman still exhorting the crowd around her to "ask important questions," the fitful horizon, the lush green forest. "Is this the earth?" he asked.

The thin man asked, "What is *earth*?"

David looked at him a long moment. "You don't understand me, do you?"

"Not so much that you'd notice," the man answered. "But I want to. I *need* to. I think you have many wonderful things to tell us. I've got this theory—it's only a theory, you understand; and what is a theory but guesswork based on logical assumptions?—and my theory has it that we have all lived *before*." He paused. "No one believes it, of course. Show us the *evidence* they tell me. But what *can* I show them? My theory isn't *based* on evidence, not in the way that—"

"I have *nothing* to tell you," David cut in. "Nothing at all." And he turned from the man and walked in the direction of the woman in the hollow. As he walked, he took notice of his bare legs and feet, then that he was wearing shoes and pants, then that there were sleeves covering his arms.

He felt pressure on his shoulder. He stopped. The thin man with the mop of unruly hair was behind him; the dark mask of his face was nodding.

"Oh, but you do have *much* to tell us. You do. You have no idea. You probably don't *know* it, but I'm here to tell you that you do; I'll lead you along."

"I'm looking for my sister," David said flatly.

"What is that?" the man asked, and his voice was filled with enthusiasm. "What is *sister*?"

"But you barely speak my language, do you," David said, as if the man's comment had been proof that there was no hope of communication. "And if I can't see your face, either—"

"You can't? I *knew* it, I *knew* it. I've always thought that you people saw us precisely the way we see you. And that's something I've talked with the others about, too, and you know what they told me—'What difference does it make?' they told me. 'What difference does it make?' Can you believe it? I mean, you people are *everywhere*. Turn around, and there you are, staring at us through all that . . . stuff." He waved his hands in front of David's face. "Do you mind if I touch it? I've always wanted to touch it." He touched David's cheek. "Aha, that's *you* under there, isn't it?" He withdrew his hand; it disappeared into the darkness that covered his own face. "Feels the same," he whispered.

"You speak in gibberish," David said, suddenly angry at the man's rambling talk.

The man would not be deterred. "It's wonderful, don't you see? You say that *I* speak in gibberish, but *I* can't say the same thing to you. You are a . . . a teacher. Do you know that?" He was close to incoherent in his enthusiasm. "I have talked to so many of you . . . faceless ones." He paused. "Does that offend you? Tell me. I've wondered. Does it offend you to be called faceless?" He shrugged. "*I* wouldn't be offended if that's what you called me. It's only a matter of perception, after all. Neither of us is actually faceless to the extent, I mean, that we have no face. Each of us does indeed have a face."

David said, looking hard into the darkness that covered the man's face, "Christ, this is like talking to a goddamned ghost."

"Ghost. Yes," the man nearly shouted. "I've heard that word. Tell me about it. Tell me about *ghost*. And *goddamned*, too. I'd like to know about that. We have people here who use that word a lot. I mean, they walk around saying *goddamned* this, and *goddamned* that—"

David cut in, "I'm sorry. I don't have the time to be your day's amusement." And again he turned away and started walking in the direction of the woman in the hollow. She was much, much closer than he remembered; he didn't remember walking that far. He was nearly one of her crowd of listeners, now. He stopped walking. He looked at her. She grew; the crowd grew, as if he were quickly drawing closer. Then she stopped growing. The crowd stopped growing. It shrank. He was at a good distance again. And he thought, *This is like walking in a dream.*

"Yes," the man said behind him. "We dream. Do *you* dream, too?" And David realized that he had said aloud what he supposed he had only been thinking. The man hurried on, "We dream of people we have never seen, and of places we have never been to. Is it the same with you, and with the people like you? Please tell me."

David felt pressure on his arm. He shook the pressure away. "Damn you, I can't even be sure any of this is *real*, for God's sake!"

"Real? Tell me about that. Tell me about *real*. Does it have to do with *reality*, and, if it does, then what is *reality*?"

"Please, leave me *alone*!" David shouted.

"Alone?" the man said. "Well, we're *all* alone, aren't we? Especially the people who choose to live in underground apartments, which is something *I'll* never understand—"

"*Damn* you!" David whispered. Was it the pain that was making him surly, he wondered, or was it was simply this maddeningly insistent man himself?

He began to weep. He had no idea why, at first. It was a spontaneous thing, as spontaneous as a sneeze, and just as unbidden. But he wept loudly; his tears stained the dry dirt path on which he and the man were walking.

He felt pressure on his arm again. He didn't resist it. He heard through his weeping and his pain, "Come with me, please. I'll make you some tea. You'll feel better in no time."

He found himself walking with the thin man, found himself only half listening—weary, pain-ridden—to the man's ramblings.

He looked back after a minute. He saw that the woman and her crowd of listeners were far, far behind, that the green mouth of the forest was gone, that the horizon was in a gray/blue turmoil, as if it were a whirlpool that was trying hard to get started.

Christian Grieg, driving on Route 96, ten miles west of Syracuse, remembered a line from a movie he'd seen several years earlier; the line was, "I am standing here beside myself." As he remembered the line, he smiled. He was no longer beside himself, was he? He was whole again. It had been a long battle, but he was whole again and he could, at last, deal with the things that the other side of him had done.

Deal with them.

Cope.

Live with.

He sighed.

Admonishing the other—hidden—side of himself for the things it had done was useless. Such acts could not be admonished—there was too much passion and too much finality in them. It was like shouting at a thunderstorm to be a little quieter.

But some of the things he had done had been what *this* side of him had done. And he had enjoyed them. Quite a lot, in fact. There was no getting around that bare, distasteful fact. He had enjoyed them. He had enjoyed that vulnerability, that pain, that fear. It had made him feel strong and important.

He jammed a fist hard into his crotch. He doubled over. The Buick swerved to the right, onto the wide shoulder. He swerved left, still doubled over, then looked up, eyes watering with pain. A small car was coming at him. He swerved right, got the Buick going straight, focused on the awful pain between his legs, relished it. "Asshole!" he screamed at himself. "Jerk! Asshole!" Then he pulled onto the shoulder and stopped the car.

When the pain was gone, he opened the glove compartment and took out a map of the area around Oneida Lake. He knew that David had a cottage there, on the lake's south side, on the Sylvan Beach Road, but he couldn't remember exactly where. It had been five years since he'd been to the cottage, after all.

He located Sylvan Beach on the map, put the map back in the glove compartment, and pulled onto the road again. He guessed that he'd be there within the hour.

Because where else would David go but to his cottage?

He had privacy there.

Memories.

Time.

NINE

It is ten years later, and Maude, who is living with her husband, Peter, in the house that once belonged to Anne Case, says to her husband, "I saw something in the upstairs hallway today." Her voice is trembling a little. She's clearly frightened by the memory of what she saw.

Peter gives her a quizzical, amused look. He doesn't want her to see that he's amused. She amuses him quite a lot with her "sensitivities" but when he has shown her that he finds her amusing, he's paid for it with many cold nights and cold glances. "Which upstairs hallway, Maude? We've got a couple of them. This is a barn we're living in, remember."

She purses her lips. She doesn't like the house referred to as a barn. She likes the house a lot. It was, in fact, only after her weeks of insistence and pleading that they decided to buy it. It had remained empty for ten years, since Anne's death, but a caretaker had seen to its upkeep, so it was move-in-able.

She says now, "It's not a barn, Peter. Please don't call it that."

He shrugs. "Sorry."

"The second floor hallway," she says. "I saw what I saw in the second floor hallway."

"Go on."

"To be truthful, I'm not sure I really saw anything."

"You're only saying that because you think it's what I think."

"I *know* what you think, Peter. Don't deceive yourself into believing that I alter my thought patterns simply to please you. I'm saying that it's possible I . . . scared myself into thinking I saw something upstairs. In fact, it's likely. In my *memory*, I see something there. In that hallway. But how reliable is that?"

"And what are you saying you saw, Maude? A ghost?"

She sighs. "I don't know. Something. It had a big . . . head. A very big head." She smiles self-consciously.

"Like E.T., you mean?"

She thinks a moment. "Maybe. Something like that. Not so pleasing as E.T., I think—"

"E.T. was hardly *pleasing*, Maude."

"I thought he was. I though he was cute."

"Uh-huh. Well, *you* probably would have. You were probably a pretty perverse little girl."

She sighs again, in annoyance. He says, "I'm sorry," and she continues, "A big head, and large eyes. Very large eyes. I think you could use the word 'bulbous' to describe his eyes."

"It was a man, then?" He stifles a smile.

She nods. "Yes. Someone . . . stocky. Mannish."

"With a very big head and bulbous eyes? Sounds charming, Maude."

"He was crying," she says.

"You used the phrase 'the earth,' " the man with the unruly light brown hair told David as they walked together. "Do you mean by that 'the ground'? I don't believe you do, and that's why I ask. I've encountered the word before, in writings, and I've decided that it has meaning. And I must know how you came to be here, too, and where it is that you will go when you're no longer here. I've seen others like you. Others without faces. I've spoken with them, but they haven't told me a thing, so . . ."

"Please don't talk," David said.

"Of course," said the man. "I understand that. People are always telling me that: 'Please keep quiet,' or 'Please don't talk,' but what can I do? I think that I've been talking forever." He paused only a moment. "*Forever*, did you hear that? I'll tell you something; it happens all the time. I use a word like that, and I don't know what in the heck it means, but I'll use it, like that, like *forever*—"

David decided to let the man ramble. Clearly, there was no way of stopping him, and just as clearly it gave the man pleasure to talk.

Ahead, halfway to the turbulent blue horizon, the particular geometry of a city was visible.

Christian Grieg turned his five-year-old Buick LeSabre onto a one-lane dirt road which, the man at the gas station had told him, would take him to Sylvan Beach Road; it skirted the south side of the lake. But it was a small lake, Christian reminded himself, and if he had to search its entire south shore until he came upon David's cottage, it would take him no more than an hour. That was no big thing.

David was his friend.

He and David had shared much, and would, doubtless, share much more.

He wanted to talk to David. He wanted to find out what David knew. He wanted to find out what David was doing and why he was doing it. He wanted to find out who David had talked to, what he had been told, and what he intended to do with what he had been told. He wanted to find out if it had any bearing on him—Christian—and, if it did, he wanted to find out how serious this whole matter really was. And, if it was serious . . .

He braked hard as a small white dog crossed in front of the car.

The dog scurried off and was gone, hidden by the high grasses to the side of the road.

Christian pushed the accelerator.

He did not want to run over a dog.

He braked again. The big car came to a bouncing stop.

He pushed his door open, got out, stood quietly on the dirt road. The afternoon was warm, pleasant. There was a little breeze and he liked it. It tickled him.

He called, "Here, doggie." But there was no response from within the tall grasses.

He walked off the road and into the grasses, calling to the dog as he moved, "Here, doggie, doggie, doggie; here, doggie doggie!"

He did not want to run over a dog today.

He found himself well off the road, found that the ground he was walking on was soft, a swamp.

He did not want to walk in a swamp today.

He turned and started back to the car.

Had he left it running? he wondered. If he had, perhaps it had been stolen. He peered over the tops of the weeds. He couldn't see the car. Damn. If it had been stolen, he would have to walk.

"Here doggie, doggie," he called. But he no longer hoped to find the dog. He knew better. The dog was, without a doubt, afraid of him. That's why it had run off. It didn't want to be run over any more than he wanted to run it over. The dog was looking out for itself, as did all natural things.

He found himself back at the road. The car was still there. It was running. No one had stolen it. Perhaps he had been overreacting to think that someone *would* steal it. The road was all but deserted, after all. Still, there were evil people everywhere. *He* knew that.

He went to the car and got in. He had left the driver's door open. He closed it, turned the ignition. The engine shut down.

He smiled. Well, wasn't that stupid! He had wanted to turn the car on, thinking it was off, but he had known—somewhere deep in his brain—that it was on, though he didn't know it consciously, so he had turned the ignition off. He'd done the same thing with light switches in lighted rooms—flicked them off thinking he had to turn them on when the light was on already.

He started the car again.

Someone was honking a horn behind him.

He turned his head, stared through the back window.

A middle-aged woman with round dark eyes and a crown of black hair was honking furiously at him to get moving on the one-lane road. He was blocking her way.

He didn't want to block anyone's way today. Nor did he want to be honked at. It was a puzzle. The two needs fought each other. To which one should he respond? he wondered.

He thought about it for a minute, while the woman in the car behind continued honking.

At last, he pushed his door open slowly, got out of the car, stared at the woman behind the wheel of the car in back of him.

She continued honking her horn. He thought he heard her curse.

He didn't want to be cursed at today, the day of his self-realization, the day he was no longer standing beside himself, the day of his naturalness.

He didn't want to be honked at, either.

He strode very quickly to the car, leaned over and looked at the middle-aged woman. The driver's window was open. He concentrated on the middle-aged woman. He didn't much like her eyes. They were shallow and meddlesome, even in anger. The inside of her car smelled of perfume, too. It was an unpleasant perfume. Lilac. It mixed with her nervous sweat and made the inside of the car smell like a place that was unsanitary.

He had written about such women as this, he remembered.

She said, "You're blocking my way. Could you *please* move." Her voice was sharp, hard to listen to. It was the voice of an unattractive bird—a crow, a starling. It was controlled and raucous at the same time.

"You're disturbing *me*," he said.

"*I'm* disturbing *you*?"

"And on this, of all days," he said.

"I don't know what in the *hell* you're talking about—" She stopped. She peered intently at him for a moment. Her expression of annoyance changed to fear as she looked into Christian's eyes. The words "Oh, my God!" escaped her in a breathy whisper and she began to furiously roll her window up.

Christian reached out and held the window two-thirds open.

The woman shook her head quickly. She was confused, he knew. And she was afraid.

"I'm sorry," he said to her. "I really am. I'm very, very sorry."

"Is the whole city like this?" David asked the thin man in the gray sportscoat and tattered white pants and unruly brown hair. They were walking a narrow street made of bricks; the close-packed two- and three-story houses all were made of wood.

Some of the houses bore the effects of several architectural influences—Victorian, Georgian, Romanesque, Modern—gingerbread and austere lines and flourishes lived together on the same house. The effect was jarring. The only unity was in the narrowness of the street and in the closeness of the houses; beyond that, there were long, rectangular windows and round windows and arched doorways and glass doorways; there were bare octagons on white walls, and fluted columns holding up nothing at all. It was as if a child possessed of too much time, too many different kinds of building blocks, and an anarchic imagination, had put the street together.

There were no people on the street, and no animals, either. David expected one or the other, or both. He expected, dimly, that there would be an open sewer on either side of the brick roadway, and garbage strewn about, flies buzzing in the warm, still air (because, if the street was reminiscent of one period and place more than another, it was of nineteenth-century London).

There were no smells, either. The air was clear and odorless.

"No," answered the thin man. "The whole city isn't like this. There are many neighborhoods."

"But where are the people?"

"In their houses, I imagine," the man said. "I think they're probably in their houses. Making love, playing games. Or they could be picnicking; do *you* picnic? Don't answer, let me guess. I'd say you do. Put together a little basketful of goodies and take it out to some green spot and fill up the tummy. People do that quite a lot here—"

"Where are you taking me?" David interrupted.

"To my apartment. It's not far. Are you getting tired? We can stop. We can sit right here on the street if you'd like."

David thought this was an odd question. Did people actually get tired here? What a ludicrous idea. He answered, "No. I'm not tired." He paused. "My head hurts."

"Hurts?"

"Yes. I have . . . a headache."

"I don't understand. Headache?"

"You don't know what pain is?"

The man shrugged. "I've seen the word used. I don't know what it means. No one does."

David stopped walking. "No one here experiences pain?"

The thin man was still walking. He stopped, looked back. David could see nothing beneath the darkness that covered his face. "I don't know if they do or don't," the man said. "I don't know what pain is. I think that I would surely *like* to know what pain is, I think that would be stimulating, and I think I would be enlightened—"

David shook his head quickly, in sudden frustration and anger. "When you fall down . . . when someone falls down and hits his elbow on the street—"

"No one falls down," the man said, and David could hear amusement in his tone.

"Do you mean that everyone is the soul of grace here? No one stumbles? No one has an accident? No one falls off a roof, or cuts his finger, or . . . or falls down?"

"Perhaps they do," the man said. "But if they do, then I haven't heard of it. And I like to keep track of things, you know. I think that I would have heard if anyone had fallen off a roof. But, of course, no one gets up on roofs to begin with. What reason would there be?" He chuckled. "It's a silly idea, getting up on a roof—I think I would have heard of *that* too—"

David—his anger and frustration mounting—said nothing as the man continued his monologue. David had merely wanted to know if what he had suspected for so long—that death was the end of pain and suffering—was true. But, ironically, this man, a resident of this place, could tell him almost nothing.

At last, David rushed forward and slapped the man hard across the face. The man stumbled backward a few feet, looked as if he were about to fall, regained his balance. His hand went up. He stood very still; his hand, where it connected to his wrist, lost itself in the darkness that covered his face.

"I'm sorry," David said. "I didn't want to do that. I had to."

The man said nothing.

David said, "Do you feel anything?" He paused. "*I* do." The palm of his hand ached from the blow.

The darkness that was the man's face moved up and down once, then again. He was nodding, David realized. But the man said nothing.

"What do you feel?" David coaxed.

The darkness moved left to right, right to left.

The man was shaking his head. "I don't know how I feel."

"It's called pain," David said.

"Is it?" The thin man's interest was piqued. "How very like a dream it is. How very much as if it is something I've experienced before. Often. This is very stimulating." He paused. "Can you do that again?"

"Hit you again?"

"Yes. I want you to. Hit me again."

"I can't. I was provoked before. I can't hit you again. I haven't got any reason to hit you again. It's not why I came here."

The man said nothing for a moment. Then he turned his body toward the wooden wall of the building near him and, without preamble, threw himself hard against it, so he hit it with his chest and his face. He bounced off the building and then onto his backside on the brick street. He sat very still. He said nothing.

David walked over to him and tried hard to peer into the darkness around his face. He saw, once more, the suggestion of large eyes and a wide nose, but this was a suggestion only, as if, again, these were features that David *expected* to see.

"Are you all right?" David asked.

The man said nothing.

"Are you hurt?" David asked.

"Hurt?" the man said. "I can't say. I don't know." He was clearly puzzled.

David reached for the man's hand to help him up.

"Volvo wagon," the man said.

David didn't understand. "Sorry?"

The man screamed the words, "Volvo wagon!" He screamed them again; there was anguish in his tone, now. "Volvo wagon! Volvo wagon!"

David backed away.

The man continued screaming the words "Volvo wagon!"

Some people appeared from the quirky houses that lined the street. They stood in their doorways, or stuck their heads out of windows and watched the man screaming "Volvo wagon!"

Eventually, all at once, the man stopped screaming and fell silent.

The people went back into their houses, or pulled their heads back into windows.

The man stood. "It's not far," he said. "But I think that the darkness will be coming soon, so we must hurry."

"Why were you yelling 'Volvo wagon'?" David asked.

The man answered, "I don't know."

"Do you know what it is?"

"What what is?"

"A Volvo wagon."

"No. What is it?"

"It's a kind of car."

"A car? I don't know what a car is."

"It's a means of transportation. Like a plane or a boat. Do you know what they are?"

"No. And I don't know what *transportation* is."

"Your feet are a means transportation."

"My feet? Is that what a Volvo wagon is? My feet?"

"No. A Volvo wagon is a kind of car. A means of transportation."

"Like my feet?"

"Yes."

"Then I don't know why I would be yelling 'Volvo wagon.' I know what my feet are. I should have been yelling 'My feet!' "

David sighed.

The sky was darkening quickly.

David said, "You don't have the faintest idea what I'm talking about, do you?"

"No," the thin man said. "But I want to." He paused. "We have to hurry."

"Why?" David asked.

"Because if we don't, then we will surely be swallowed up by the darkness."

It's ten years later, and Peter, the man who has moved into the house that once belonged to Anne Case, says to his wife, Maude, "Have you seen any more of our friend with the big head and bulbous eyes?" Peter is smiling as he says it, but he supposes that Maude can't see him smile because they're lying in bed and the light is off.

There's a moment's silence, then Maude says, "No." A short pause. "I've decided that I really didn't see anything."

"Oh?"

"Or perhaps if I did see something . . ." A pause. A sigh. "I've given this a lot of thought, Peter, and I've decided that if I *did* see something then it was probably not a man at all. I think it would have to have been a woman." A pause. "The woman who lived here. Anne Case." Another pause. She had been on her side, facing away from her husband. She rolled to her back. "And because she was murdered . . . I mean, that's quite traumatic, isn't it?"

"Quite."

"So, as traumatic as it was, her spirit is forever earthbound. Tied for an eternity to this house, to the place where she was murdered. Unable to find peace. It's very sad, Peter, but it's probably happened a million times. Someone dies violently and their soul simply can't . . . pass over. To the other side, I mean."

"Why?"

"Why? It's obvious, isn't it? I shouldn't have to tell you why." A short pause. "And when I saw her, I simply . . . misinterpreted what I was seeing. It's not every day you see a ghost, so I guess I was a little shaken by it. The whole thing couldn't have lasted more than two or three seconds, anyway. One moment he was there and the next moment he . . . she . . . whatever, was gone."

"Poof!"

"Yes. Poof!"

TEN

The elderly man—a widower—lived by himself on Sylvan Beach, in a three-bedroom cottage that he and his late wife had shared for twenty years, ever since their retirement from the motel business.

The car that was stopped ahead of him on the narrow dirt road looked familiar. He thought he remembered seeing it a couple of times in the past few weeks; it wasn't easy to miss. Most people in the area drove big American cars. This was a Toyota. Blue. Sparkling in the late afternoon sun.

He stopped his car a couple of feet behind the Toyota. He could see the back of the driver's head—a crown of dark hair sticking not far above the headrest. He thought he remembered seeing this driver, too, once or twice at the Sylvan Beach Grocery. She was the only woman in the area who had such a crown of black hair.

Why was she stopped here? he wondered. Perhaps her car wouldn't start. Perhaps she had just braked for an animal—the area was a popular crossing for all kind of animals; feral cats, dogs, deer, woodchucks, oppossums—and the road, in summer, was often littered with their dead bodies. Perhaps she had actually hit something and was in shock behind the wheel of her Toyota.

The elderly man was in a quandary as to what to do. There wasn't a lot of room to maneuver around the Toyota, and he didn't want to honk his horn for fear of seeming rude. If someone came up behind him, he'd explain the situation and hope that they would be as patient as he was. But it was unlikely that anyone would come along. The road was not much used this time of year because most of the cottages on the lake were seasonal. The summer people weren't due to show up for a couple of months.

He waited for a minute, two minutes, five minutes. It was not an inordinately long amount of time for him to wait. He often relinquished his place in various lines (at theaters and grocery stores and the motor vehicle department) to people who looked as if they were in a much bigger hurry than he was—or told him they were—and had waited sometimes fifteen minutes or a half hour longer than he otherwise would have. So, five minutes was nothing. But, still, this woman sitting so quietly in her car was something of a puzzle. She might be hurt. She might have had some kind of attack. Maybe she was simply daydreaming and would get moving soon enough.

The thin man opened the front door to his apartment house and held it so David could go in.

But David did not go in. He wasn't sure he trusted this man, or that he trusted anything, here. This place was simply too real. It should have been illusory, it should have been more like a dream; the streets he walked here should have been malleable beneath—brick or asphalt or stone, these streets should have felt like sand or water beneath his feet; but they were solid and unyielding; and the buildings were hard-edged and well delineated against the ever-changing sky. They, like the sky, should have changed, however subtly, with each passing second. This was, after all—as he had always believed—only a land of dreams, no more than a place where fantasies were allowed to come true, where childhoods were relived and relived again, where the best and happiest moments of a billion different completed lives were replayed endlessly.

This was a place of reward, a place of rest and peace and harmony. It existed only because its inhabitants *allowed* it to exist.

"Go in," invited the thin man, gesturing with his hand toward the inside of the apartment building. "It may not be heaven, but it's home."

David shook his head. "I can't. I'm afraid."

The man shook his head. David saw only the darkness framing it move. "I don't understand what *afraid* is. I want to, certainly."

David did not answer him. Christian, he realized at once, had been right. His first visit here, five years ago, when he had nearly drowned, had really shown him almost nothing. He had seen so very little of this place, and his fantasies had filled in what he had not seen. He had devised a clever, enticing fiction, a heaven of his own making, a heaven, an afterlife—whatever you wanted to call it—that would have pleased *him*. And it apparently had nothing to do with reality.

This was reality.

This squat brick apartment building, this thin man who talked almost ceaselessly and whose face was covered in darkness, these hard streets, this always-changing sky, this strange little city whose houses seemed to have been built from memories that were incomplete.

Here, *he* was the ghost, *he* was the one who was unreal, *he* was the fantasy.

"Go in," the man said again. "And don't be afraid. There are no ghosts." A brief pause. "There I go again. *Ghosts*. Who knows what ghosts are? It's like *forever*, isn't it? And . . . and *microwave*, *Reddenbacher*, *World War One*, all little snippets of nothing, motes of dust—"

Beyond the front door, there were dark stairs and a darker hallway.

"Are we going up?" David asked, interrupting the thin man's monologue.

"We're going to have some tea," said the man. "Our walk has made me very thirsty."

A dog ran loose on the rocky beach of Oneida Lake, near the Sylvan Beach Road. The dog was lost. The night before, she had chased a rabbit into the fields near her home and then, because her sense of smell was not what a dog's sense of smell should be, she had not been able to find her way back.

The dog was small, white, skittish. Her owners called her "Tootie." Every few moments, she glanced over her shoulder. She was looking for two things—her owners, and other dogs that roamed freely in the area. Two of those dogs had chased her until her lungs were close to bursting.

ELEVEN

Karen read:

Dearest Anne,
Do you know what I give to the world when I'm writing? I give it myself. It's that simple. I go inside myself and I pull out all the creatures that exist there, all the passions, all the desperation to be real, all the good and evil, and I make people out of them to populate the books that I write.

And so, dear Anne, I have come to realize the necessity of self-knowledge, and the real danger in self-ignorance, the enormous treachery of keeping our inner and outer selves separate.

We cannot for long safely allow our demon inner selves expression only in our dreams.

You understand that too well because you are the person you

The letter ended there. It was written in black fountain pen; many of the upstrokes and downstrokes were obscured by flares of ink.

I shouldn't have been snooping, Karen thought, and tucked the unfinished letter back into the copy of Christian's first novel, *Greed,* where she had found it.

She closed her eyes, felt tears starting. My God, he'd never mentioned having had a relationship with Anne Case. Not once. Her name had hardly passed his lips except in conversation with David.

The implications of what she was thinking astounded her. Frightened her.

She looked again at the copy of Christian's first novel which had been the letter's hiding place. She withdrew it again slowly from the bookcase, flipped the pages. There were no other errant pieces of paper, no other letters.

She put the book back where she'd found it.

Perhaps the "Anne" that the letter referred to wasn't Anne Case at all. Perhaps the letter was simply a piece of fiction, part of a new manuscript. Perhaps the Anne referred to was another Anne. There had been no date on the letter, so it was impossible to tell how old it was. And it was unsigned, too, so it was impossible to say definitely that Christian had even written it.

She shook her head miserably. Of course he'd written it. The handwriting had been his, the style of writing had been his—intense and circuitous; of course he'd written it.

There was another copy of *Greed* standing next to the one she had looked through. She pulled it from the bookcase, hesitated, flipped through it.

The pages opened at once to several folded

pieces of paper stuck between pages 102 and 103. She lifted the sheets out. She unfolded them. They were written in a small, meticulous hand—not Christian's bold strokes.

She read:

He's a chameleon. Many people are. But he's especially good at it. His whole countenance changes, not just his skin. And, unlike a chameleon, he changes it at will, at the necessity of the moment, and of the conquest to be made.

He professed to know me and understand me. Perhaps he did. I *believed* that he did, and it made me feel . . . hopeful. But even if he did, or didn't, there is the fact of himself, the fact that he is a monster, the fact that I have slept with a monster. Thank God I cannot bear children.

"No more," I told him. He professed to understand. He said that I had misinterpreted him and though that was an injustice, he would overlook it, that he understood me, and understood why I had misinterpreted him. He would forgive me immediately, he said.

"For all the tomorrows we will have," he said, "I will forgive you now for this injustice you have committed against me." He said this smilingly, and his eyes were a little moist as if he were overcome by the emotion of the moment. It was an act, of course. One of his chameleon changes.

"No, I don't believe you," I told him. "I believed you before. Too many times. I don't believe you now. This is over." And I wanted to add, "I'm sorry." But I didn't, because I was glad it was over. Our two weeks together were history and I was ecstatic. And troubled, too. Because I could see that he would not let go. Perhaps he *could not* let go. I had disarmed him, seen him for himself, exposed him. I was his enemy. I had to be bested, and he was going to do it.

"You think you know me," he said. "Perhaps you do. Perhaps you know as much as anyone . . . *more* than anyone. But you don't know enough, my love." I cringed when he called me that. It wasn't always so, but it was then. The phrase "my love" was, from his lips, something malodorous. I wondered, suddenly, how much anyone knew him, how significantly he had fooled everyone else in his life. Or was I somehow more vulnerable, and naïve?

But I am not naïve, and I am not vulnerable. My illness has shown me that I am more than flesh and blood. My soul dances around me, bold and ashamed at the same time, quivering and bold and frightened all at the same time. I am spirit, mostly, and spirit cannot be bested.

It is something I dearly want to believe. That my spirit—that part of me that is not bone and muscle—cannot be bested.

I told him, "You want to hurt me."

He said, "I don't want to hurt you. I want to show you myself. What's wrong with that? It's only natural and good that I want to show my true self to the woman that I love."

"You have," I said. "You've shown me yourself. I hate what you've shown me. It's awful. It's monstrous."

His smile went away for a moment. He didn't like me telling him he was a monster, and that was clear.

He said, "Monster mean's antinature, it means perversion, it means something abhorrent, something unintended by God—"

I told him to leave. He refused. I told him that I would call the police if he didn't leave. He still refused. I picked up the phone, pretended to dial. He laughed. He knew I was pretending. He's a very smart man. I put the phone down.

He was besting me already, and I knew it. So did he.

I said to him, "Someday you're going to hurt me. How can I allow that?" And I picked up the phone again. And in his full view I dialed the number for the police.

He came over immediately and grabbed my wrist very hard. He let go of it almost at once, as if the act had shocked him. Indeed, he *looked* shock for a moment. Then he smiled again. The same sort of smile. His eyes moist.

He let go of my wrist and looked silently at me for a very long time. He smiled as he looked. The same smile. Same moist eyes. The eyes of a monster.

And at last he said, "*I* am a whole person, my love." Then he left the house.

For a long while, Karen stared silently, disbelievingly at the sheets of paper in her hand.

She felt suddenly numb. She felt as if she would scream.

The elderly man had pulled around the blue Toyota, had stopped a couple of feet in front of it, and now was looking in the Toyota's driver's window. He knew that the woman in the front seat was dead. Her face was buried in the seat; he could see only her luxurious crown of black hair, and he could smell the lilac perfume that had been splashed all around the inside of the car. But he knew the woman was dead because her left arm—

the right was beneath her—hung over the front of
the seat at an odd angle, so her palm was facing
him, and he thought he could see blood here and
there—on her gray coat, on the floor, on the seat
itself. He also knew she was dead because he had
a *sense* of such things. He had watched his wife
die, and his best friend; his daughter, very recently; his mother. He knew about death and how
it sat so leadenly on people. There was no doubt
of it. He didn't have to reach in and check her
pulse. This poor woman was dead.

He sighed. The woman wouldn't be able to
watch her grandchildren grow, if she had any;
she'd never become a great-grandparent, as he
was, would never be able to really appreciate what
a long life can give to a person—the richness of
memories and the wisdom and harmony of age,
and a willingness—even an eagerness—to leave
this life for something that was doubtless worlds
better. All of that had been taken from her. And
that, more than simply the act of violence which
had been committed against her, was a real crime.

Poor woman.

The elderly man put his hand on the bottom of
the open driver's window. The metal felt very cold,
icy cold. But then, everything felt cold to him these
days.

He was sorry for this woman because she would
grow no older. He was glad for this woman because she had left the earth behind.

He was envious of this woman.

He took his hand off the driver's window. He
went back to his car, got in, drove to his cottage
three miles down Sylvan Beach Road, and called
the Sheriff's Department.

There were no lights illuminating the stairway
looming in front of him, and David was afraid.

The metal steps disappeared into darkness halfway to the second floor.

He put his hand tentatively on the wood banister. It was warm to the touch, as if other hands
had been on it very recently.

David said to the thin man, "I'm sorry. I can't
go up there."

The man, standing just behind him, asked,
"Something's preventing you from going up
there?"

David nodded. "My fear."

The man, surprising David, said nothing.

"You don't understand fear, do you?" David
asked, his gaze still on the dark stairway above
him.

"I don't understand the word," the man answered, and started to elaborate, when David interrupted.

"Then you don't understand the concept." He
took his hand off the banister, backed up a step,
toward the thin man, felt the man back away, too.
"I can see that there is much that survives death,"
David said. "Language, for instance." He turned,
stared into the darkness that was the man's face.
It was framed by the light coming in the open door
just behind him. "So if you don't understand the
word *fear*, then the concept died with you." He
stepped quickly around the man and headed for
the doorway. "I'm sorry. I can't talk with you. This
isn't why I came here." He closed his eyes against
a sudden onslaught of pain. "This isn't at all why
I came here."

The thin man watched David leave the building
and, when David was down the street a bit, went
to the doorway and called after him, "You'll want
a place to be when the light is gone. Being on these
streets when darkness comes is foolhardy indeed."

David stopped walking.

He looked back.

For an instant, a breath, he saw the man's face. Wide nose, large, closely set eyes, underslung jaw. Then it was lost in shadow again and David easily convinced himself that he had seen nothing more than his own mental construction of the man's face.

David shouted, "I'll take that chance."

"I'm sorry?" The man said.

"I said I'll take my chances."

"Chances? There are none," the man shouted.

"Good," David said, misunderstanding him, and went on his way in search of his sister, Anne, though he had no idea where to begin.

In the room in the house without doors, a woman wept. She looked to be in her early sixties, heavyset, black-haired. Her weeping was soft and unself-conscious. While she wept she also smiled. Eventually, her smile changed to laughter and her weeping grew more intense, so she was laughing and crying at the same time.

The woman was new to this place. She had come into the house, and into the room, because it was familiar, as were weeping and laughter, and she desperately needed the familiar.

Eventually, her weeping and laughing subsided.

TWELVE

Karen Duffy could not ignore the fact of the pages that had been squirreled away in a copy of Christian's first novel, nor the fact of his letter hidden in another copy of the same novel. Certainly there had to be more. Certainly this man she had professed to love was hiding something. Clearly it was not, as she had first thought, something heinous. (How could it be? She knew him well enough to know that he was incapable of anything more than simple anger or rudeness.) Clearly it was something mundane—a love affair that had probably ended long ago, when it would have been none of her business, anyway.

The fact that Anne Case had been brutally murdered had no bearing on her relationship with Christian.

Clear enough.

She did not read the poems and letters she

found hidden around the house, in other copies of Christian's nine books. She merely scanned a few lines of each poem or letter, and then set it down—poems here, letters there.

She would read everything thoroughly later.

And maybe then she'd be able to make sense of it all.

"His name is David Case," Christian said to the woman gardening. He had pulled his car to the side of the road and was talking to the woman from the driver's seat, his window rolled down. "And I know he has a cottage around here some-where. I've been there, in fact." Christian gave her an embarrassed grin. "But that was some time ago, and for the life of me I can't remember—"

"I know of no one named Case," the woman said. She was thin and square-faced; she wore a blue spring jacket and gray pants, and as she talked to him, she sat on her haunches and looked at what she was doing—removing rocks from her garden—rather than at Christian. Her tone was brusque. "And I know most of the people who live on Sylvan Beach."

Christian grinned thinly at her. "Thanks, any-way," he said, and drove off.

Why couldn't he remember where David's cot-tage was? he wondered. He'd been there not too long ago. Five years. But all he could remember of it was the living room, which was narrow and oblong and claustrophobic; the kitchen, not much larger than a phone booth—it was alive with fat brown spiders—and the rocky, precipitous lake-front. He couldn't remember the cottage's facade; perhaps it was much like most of the cottages here—small and squat and pleasantly painted beige or light blue or yellow.

Green.

It was green.

He remembered suddenly.

Green. White shutters.

Or white with green shutters.

He slowed the Buick around a hard curve. Cattails crowded the narrow road on either side.

He pulled the car left, into a narrow lane bordered on both sides by swamp. He stopped fifty
feet down the lane. The car was not easily seen
here by another car coming from either direction.

David thought of calling his sister's name. In
this magical place, perhaps she would hear him
no matter where she might be, even if she were
miles away, thousands of miles away. They would
be connected by their love for each other; she
would hear him, and they would be reunited, however briefly.

Long enough, clearly, for his questions to be answered.

Why had she been murdered?

Had she found peace and happiness at last?

Who was her murderer?

He opened his mouth to call to her. He stayed
silent.

This place wasn't magical at all, was it? He had
expected that it would be magical. He had expected that it would be a land of dreams. But it
wasn't.

It wasn't *heaven*.

Heaven was the place he had constructed in his
own fantasies, the place that legend had built up
for him over the years he had been alive on earth.

This wasn't heaven.

This was . . .

Something in between.

There were people around him on the narrow street. They were moving slowly. Some were talking to themselves or to people walking with them. Their talk was, variously, animated, quiet, loud; what he could hear of the conversations going on made little sense—there were references to animals, to cold, to summer and, several times, to the darkness, and, once, to "the small creatures of the darkness." But he could not hear whole sentences. He caught snippets of sentences, phrases out of context.

Some of the people apparently turned their heads his way, but he could see no faces. A man appeared to give David a friendly nod and David nodded back, thinking how ludicrous the exchange was—two faceless creatures nodding to one another.

The people around him were dressed in varying ways (though it seemed to make little difference how one was dressed; the air was neither warm nor cold; it was much like water that has been heated to body temperature). A few wore what looked like cold-weather clothes—several layers of loose clothing, or clothes that looked like coats without buttons or pockets—and others wore very little. Short pants. Long sleeveless shirts. What looked like loose summer dresses made of a very thin cloth.

The bodies he saw—those that were not dressed in cold-weather clothes—were the bodies of men and women and children, and they were invariably healthy looking and nicely developed. Genitalia and sexual parts were much in evidence; penises peeked out from beneath short pants, breasts from the generous openings at the sides of shirts; bottoms twinkled in the bright daylight from beneath long shirts which moved up and down in time with walking.

David thought, *There is no shame here*. He didn't like the thought, didn't like himself for thinking it.

Why should there be shame *here*, of all places?

"You have to come back with me," David heard.

He whirled. The man who had brought him to this city was behind him. For a moment, half a breath, David saw his face. Wide nose. Large eyes. Dark brown skin.

David said, "What I *have* to do is find my sister."

The darkness that was the thin man's face moved left and right. "I don't understand that. *Sister*." A pause. "Darkness will come. You'll want to be inside for it. If you're not inside then I can't be responsible for the consequences, believe me—"

"When?" David cut in.

"When?" the man asked.

"When does the darkness come?"

"I don't understand that either," the man said. "*When*."

"Within the hour?" David explained. "In a few minutes? It's very simple." He could feel his temper flaring. "When does the damned *darkness* come?" He looked up, toward the sun.

But there was no sun. There was only white light, and an ever-changing sky.

"Where's the sun?" he asked.

The thin man said that he did not understand this either.

"The *sun*, goddammit!" David shouted. He grabbed the man's shirt collar, drew the man close. "The *sun*. It's part of the damned *solar system*, which is part of the damned *galaxy*, which is part of the damned *universe*!"

"I don't know," the man said without emotion.

His breath smelled strongly of onions. "Perhaps we could talk about it. I would very much like to talk about it. I have things to show you . . ." The man stopped talking in midsentence.

Around them, the light was quickly beginning to fade.

Did she have them all? wondered Karen Duffy. All the poems and letters (unfinished letters) and little, odd pieces of fiction (were they fiction?). She had looked everywhere, in all of the books that Christian himself had written, and in most of the other books, too. She had found that he had hidden nothing in the other books. These unfinished letters he had written and the things that Anne Case had written were very personal, so he had chosen a very personal hiding place for them. His own books.

But wasn't he afraid that a visitor—her, for instance?—would find them?

Or had he somehow wanted them to be found?

She had the poems and the fiction in one pile, the letters in another, on a coffee table in front of her. The piles were high—almost thirty pages of letters, she guessed, perhaps thirty or forty pages of poems and fiction (if it was fiction).

She'd unfolded them, laid them out neatly, and now she was looking bemusedly at them, finding interest, for the moment, only in the ink Christian had used—black fountain pen—and in the small, meticulous hand that Anne used. Nothing was typed, and that didn't surprise Karen. After ten books, Christian still did not use a typewriter for his first drafts. He always wrote them in longhand. "It's closer to the blood and sinew," he had told her.

She picked up one of Anne's poems and started reading.

* * *

"Very sturdy-looking man," the woman said to Fred Collins. She'd been jogging on the street in front of Anne's house, and Collins, taking a chance, had stopped her to ask if she jogged there often. Yes, she had told him. She jogged there practically every day, and every evening, too. She lived only a mile away, on Hyacinth Crescent. She jogged five miles a day, up Hyacinth Crescent—a half mile—to Forest Drive, to Poplar Ridge—another mile—and finally here, to Troy Road. Collins then had identified himself, explained his purpose for being at the house, asked if she had ever seen anything unusual as she jogged past. She didn't know what he meant by unusual, she said; perhaps he meant had she seen any men coming and going from the house. She had. She remembered one man in particular. "A stocky man. Square-faced. Not really good-looking so much as sturdy-looking. A very sturdy-looking man. Very . . . mannish-looking, if you follow me."

"And you say that you saw no one else but this man?" Collins asked now.

She shook her head. "I didn't say that. There *was* another man. A young man. But I saw him only once. A month or so before the murder, I think."

"Could you describe him?"

She nodded. "He was young, as I said. Average height. Average build." She paused. "Rather pale, I remember. Almost unhealthy-looking."

Brian Fisher, Collins realized. The woman was clearly describing Brian Fisher, whom David Case had said had been Anne's lover, and who had probably been at the house often.

But who was the other man? The stocky, mannish-looking one?

"Do you remember the car that the stocky man was driving?" Collins asked.

She shook her head. "I'm not good with cars. It was gray. Silver. Monotone, anyway. A big car, I think."

"But you couldn't say what make?"

"I'm sorry, no."

The tall, thin man was running. David was running behind him. David felt the brick street hit the soles of his feet and found it oddly reassuring. As he ran, he found the caress of air moving over his face reassuring, too. The dull ache in his side, his lungs straining for oxygen, the sound of his own voice—"Where are we going? Why are we running?"—all of it was oddly reassuring, oddly comforting.

And yet he could sense fear all around him. From the man ahead. From within the houses, where the people walking had retreated when the light had begun to fade.

Fear? he wondered.

Was it fear? Were they—the people in the houses, the man running—afraid?

Of what?

"Why are we running, dammit?"

"The darkness," the man called back, and David remembered a phrase he had heard very recently—*the small creatures of darkness.* His brain flashed a quick and awful picture of thousands of rodentlike animals moving like oil over the brick streets, devouring everything in their path.

The small creatures of darkness.

Rats. A *plague* of rats!

He was convinced.

He ran faster. He caught up with the man ahead of him and shouted, "Rats?"

"Darkness!" the man shouted back. "Us."

"Us?" David shouted.

"Darkness," the man shouted. "We're running from the darkness. It's all right. We run, it follows. Just keep running, one foot in front of the other, arms pumping, air moving in, air moving out. . . ."

THIRTEEN

"Have we got far to go?" David shouted.

"To where?" the man shouted back. Together, they turned a corner that led to what appeared, in the darkness, to be a narrower street. Apparently, it was unpaved, because David could feel the earth give a little beneath him as he ran.

"To your apartment," David shouted.

"I don't know," the man shouted.

"Isn't that ..." David was getting short of breath. "Isn't that where we're going?"

"To my apartment?"

"Yes." David was breathing heavily.

"We're running from the darkness," the man called.

"Shit!" David wheezed.

"Away from the darkness," the man repeated, and David could hear that he, too, seemed out of breath.

Far ahead, David saw what looked like daylight illuminating the tops of the city's taller buildings.

Christian Grieg thought that his life was starting now. For its first forty years, who had he been? A stranger to himself. Someone who had tried to hide in his books. And reveal himself there, too. But doing that was a sign not so much of weakness (though it *was* that) as of dishonesty. A person must go into the universe *knowing* himself, and *being* himself—reacting to the world in the way that the world (nature) *intended* him to react, not the way society—*other people*—had programmed him to react. That was dishonest. That was a lie. It was a crime against himself, against nature, against the *universe*!

Oh, this was a happy day in a life filled with unhappy days, a life filled with self-deception. A happy day of self-knowledge and fulfillment.

He was being *himself* without constraint, acting upon the dictates of his nature without constraint.

Nature was without. *He* was without. *He* was nature.

He was the world's first truly natural being since the time of cavemen.

But he was better. He had *intelligence* as well as naturalness.

How very like a God he was. How very like

he would go into the universe untainted, and the universe would accept him with great happiness, and all the others, so tentatively populating the universe with him, would know him and love him and realize that it was not their place to *forgive* him because *forgiveness* could not figure into the scheme of this—one does not forgive the black widow spider, or the cobra, or the lion because it acts naturally he did not require forgiveness from the woman with the crown of black hair he did not require forgiveness from Anne Case

he was a whole, natural being in a world filled with weaklings and dishonesty, and he did not require forgiveness from anyone, save from himself for being at variance with the universe for so long

for his whole life practically until

now

here

he was a whole man a whole man a whole man a whole

man a

David could hear movement from behind him as he ran. He thought that it must be very loud if he could hear it above his breathing and the clop-clop of his feet—and the breathing and the clop-clop of the feet of the man running just ahead of him.

He was hearing what sounded very much like a steady wind, or rushing water.

It was clear to him. He was hearing the plague of rats he had conjured up in his imagination. They were behind him, *just* behind him on that narrow, black street, in the darkness. They were at his heels, and the tap-tap of their millions of tiny feet was what he was hearing above the sound of his breathing and his own feet. The scrabbling of their tiny claws on the earth (or the pavement, or the brick) made a sound like wind or rushing water.

He did not want to look back. He knew that if he did he would see nothing. Only darkness. The light was ahead. He could see it illuminating the tops of the city's taller buildings. There were spires, like the tops of churches, there were flat roofs on brick buildings, there were clocks—they seemed to be clocks; perhaps there were no hands, or no numbers, but they were in the shape of clocks—and all of these building were illuminated.

The *light* was there.

And that's why this man was running. This man *knew* this place and so he was running for the light.

And behind . . .

David looked.

He saw darkness.

He wanted to scream at the darkness. He didn't. Instead, he yelled, "Something's behind us!"

And the man running ahead of him yelled back, "Us! The darkness!"

Then there was light again.

Christian Grieg saw the curve of the small lake, three dozen small lake-houses, movement here and there, caused either by the wind, or by animals— chipmunks, muskrats, squirrels finding their way to bird feeders that would, inevitably, be empty, because the summer people had yet to arrive.

The scene was blue and green and white-blue— the lake, the earth, and the sky—punctuated by the colors of the little lake-houses, square and rectangular shapes of yellow, light blue, brown. The wind moved the lake and gave it life.

It was a very cheerful scene. Christian enjoyed it. He smiled crookedly.

Karen Duffy whispered, "Your poems are not very good, Anne, I'm sorry." But the poems of only a few people were very good, weren't they?

These poems were simply not enjoyable. Anne Case had been an unhappy woman, that was clear. And these poems were unhappy. Who could genuinely enjoy another person's unhappiness?

Karen knew that she was weeping. It wasn't the poems that were making her weep, it was what they told her—along with Christian's letters— about the man she had spent so much time with.

That he was insane.

"We have no reason to run anymore," the man said to David, and stopped running.

David stopped. For a moment, he could clearly see the man's face—the wide nose, large eyes, strong jaw, dark brown skin. Then it was lost in shadow again.

David looked behind him where, in the darkness, he had heard the sound of wind or rushing water.

He saw the dirt street, the close buildings— stucco, brick, wood, all with many tall windows— and he saw the moving sky above.

"What was it?" he asked.

"Us," said the thin man. "Darkness." The man had seemed out of breath for a moment, but now did not.

"I mean that sound. Like wind."

"The small creatures of the darkness," the man said. "Us."

"No. Rats," David whispered.

"Rats?" the man asked.

"Were they rats?"

"They were the small creatures of darkness."

"Were they like rats?"

"What are rats?"

"Have you ever *seen* them?"

"Do you mean have I seen rats?"

"No. These creatures of darkness. Have you ever actually seen them?"

What sounded like a quick chuckle came from the thin man. "How could I have seen them? They only come out in the dark. What can anyone see

in the dark? You look and all you see is little mov-
ing bits of light, and you know what those are?
Spots. Like the things you see when you wake up.
Spots. Dust in the eye—"

David sighed. "Then what do they do?"

"What do what do?"

"These small creatures of the darkness. For
God's sake, what have we been talking about?"

"No one knows."

"Then why do you run from them?"

"Because I don't *know* what they might do."

"Do you think they'll hurt you?"

"I don't know. Everyone has always run toward
the light in the darkness. And we have heard the
small creatures of the darkness behind us as we
ran."

David thought that talking with this man was
like talking in code. He asked, "How do you know
that they're small?"

The man answered, "I don't. I don't know anything about them. They could easily be very large
creatures of the darkness, I suppose; they could
easily be the size of refrigerators, or, or . . . stoves
and refrigerators, but that's unlikely isn't it. I
mean, we'd *hear* them—"

"But you said they were *us*," David cut in.

"Did I? I don't remember."

"And you don't know what they do?"

"No one does."

"And you've never seen them?"

"That's right."

"Then how do you know they exist at all?"

There was a moment's silence. Then the man
said, "I don't understand. They *exist* in the darkness; what is to know or not know?" Again David
heard what he thought was a quick chuckle.
"Come now," the man said, and the darkness that
covered his face nodded toward where they had

just come from. "Let's go back to my apartment. I have a trillion things to show you."

Fred Collins couldn't feel Anne Case in her house anymore. It saddened him. The house was simply a place where a particularly heinous murder had been committed, and the woman who had lived here, and died here, had been swept away.

And she had been swept from his thoughts and his fantasies, as well. This saddened him, too. Communicating with her ghost—her memory— had been a very pleasant diversion. Now it didn't work. When he tried to talk with her, she didn't answer or even turn her head toward him. The house didn't echo with her footfalls. Her perfume no longer lingered in the air.

It never had, he realized. He had wanted it to, had willed it to, but it never had.

The house was empty of Anne Case.

His brain was empty of her.

It happened.

People and events came and went and intermingled and were gone.

There was nothing anyone had ever been able to do about it.

FOURTEEN

The thin man invited David to sit in a ladder-back chair near the apartment's only window, which looked out on the street two stories below. The man asked if David would like some tea.

David sat in the ladder-back chair. "Tea?" he asked, thinking the offer was very odd. "You drink tea here?"

"We drink tea everywhere," the man answered. He was standing at what looked like a white porcelain stove at the far end of the large room. To David's left there was a small bed, neatly made with a fluffy pillow and a brightly colored quilt. At the foot of the bed—which was itself made of what looked like tubular black metal—there was a small chest of drawers. A rectangular mirror in a wooden frame stood on top.

The man held up an ornate teakettle that looked

like it was made of brass. "Orange pekoe tea," he said.

"Orange pekoe," David said, still thinking that the whole idea of sharing tea with this faceless man was somehow absurd.

"Yes, orange pekoe," the man said, apparently mistaking David's remark for a question.

"Thank you, no," David said.

"No tea?" The man sounded put off.

"I'm not thirsty," David said.

"Thirsty?"

"I don't need any tea right now. Thank you."

"Thank you," the man said, and set the teakettle on the stove. He went wordlessly to a large bookcase standing against the wall not far from the stove. The bookcase was lined, floor to top, with what looked like manuscripts. The man took one of the manuscripts down, held it in his hands for a moment as if he were reading it, then turned his head toward David. "I would like you to read this and tell me what it means." He crossed the room and put the thick manuscript—bound with twine—on David's lap. The manuscript was untitled and written in longhand, in red ink, on plain yellowish paper. The handwriting was very small. David glanced at the manuscript, then up at the faceless man, who was apparently looking down at him.

David said, "I didn't come here to read."

The man said nothing for a moment. Then the darkness that was his face turned briefly toward the window, then abruptly back to David, who realized, all at once, that the man was nervous. "Read a little of it," the man pleaded. "A few sentences, a page—I don't care. Just get the sense of it, give *me* the sense of it, and I'll be happy, and you'll be happy—"

David shook his head. "I didn't come here to read," he repeated. "I came here to find my sister."

A sigh came from the darkness covering the man's face. "Sister," he said, "mother/father. It's all in there." He reached, tapped the manuscript with a long, dark finger. "I need to know what they mean. You can *tell* me what they mean."

"Tell you what what means? Sister?"

"Sister, mother/father."

"You want to know what sister, mother, and father mean?"

The darkness that was the man's face bobbed. "Oh, yes. Yes, I do."

He smiled. David could see his smile, could see his large eyes, wide nose, his smiling, full mouth. Then darkness covered the man's face again.

"I saw you then," he said.

David said, "Saw me?"

"Your face. Very briefly. It may be significant; of what, I don't know—transition, transmigration, transportation; my God, my God all these words ricochetting about in my head . . ." He rambled on.

David didn't interrupt him.

As the man talked, David read the first few sentences of the manuscript to himself. They were:

In enee timwe love, thair ispast, groathand here we are here we are.
The gray eyes sweeeepoavar, caress. Guodbie, thaysae.

David looked up at the thin man. The man stopped talking at once and apparently looked back. "I don't know what this means," David said. "It's gibberish." He looked at the manuscript again. He reread the first two sentences. They made more sense the second time around. In large part, they were phonetically written, he realized. These people obviously came to this place with their language and writing abilities intact, but with limitations. There was probably no formal instruction in language here.

David read the sentences slowly, aloud: "In any time we love, there . . . is past . . ." He stopped, studied the next word hard, then continued, "Growth and here we are, here we are." He looked up at the thin man. "I'm sorry. It's still gibberish to me." He looked at the second sentence, read aloud: "The gray eyes . . ." He paused, continued. "The gray eyes sweep over. Caress. Goodbye, they say." He sighed. "Yes, I know what this means," he told the faceless man. "The second sentence anyway." He paused. "This talks about someone who has died, apparently—"

"Died?"

"Yes." David paused. How could this man understand what death was? "You don't know what I'm talking about, do you?"

The darkness that covered the man's face moved slowly from side to side. The man said, "But I want to. I *need* to." He paused. "I think if all of us knew what words like these really meant, we would be . . ." He paused. "*Died*, of course," he went on, as if in sudden revelation, "demised, mortified, denuded, passed on, bequested, requested, R-S-V-P'd." He paused again. "No," he admitted, "I don't understand a word of it."

David sighed again. "This is why you asked me here? So I could read this book?"

"All of it. Yes. From cover to cover and from page to page, while we drink our orange pekoe tea, you know, and discuss conundrums aplenty, oh yes—"

"So I can tell you what sisters and mothers and fathers are?"

"Yes. And more. Lots more, tons more—"

"I don't need to read this book to tell you that."

"You don't?"

David stood, manuscript in hand, and took it back to the bookcase. He turned his head, looked at the faceless man. "Do you know where I came from?"

"Came from?"

"Yes. Before I came here."

The faceless man said nothing.

David sighed. "I'm sorry, my friend. I don't think I can tell you a thing."

Green with white shutters. Christian remembered, now. *Green. White shutters.*

White shutters.

Green.

Green.

Walls.

Green walls and white shutters would certainly be easy to spot along this shoreline, as easy as spotting flies on a cake, on a pig, flies flying circus
clouds
cloudless day this day of salvation my salvation my salvation my salvation my salvation my salvation flies green shutters white
shutters green walls

Christian remembered now.

But there was no house with white shutters and green walls. There were brown houses, blue houses, yellow houses with green shutters, green shutters and white walls. He could see them all laid out along the shoreline, like Monopoly houses, to infinity.

He decided that he would walk the shoreline.

He knew that before long he would find David that way.

The faceless man asked, "Why can you tell me nothing?"

"Because," David answered, "very simply, we don't speak the same language."

"But we do. It's obvious. I speak, you hear, you respond; you talk, I listen, I respond; vice versa and over and over again—"

"We use the same words," David broke in. "Approximately." He paused, then went on, "If I were to tell you that I was dying, right now, as we speak, would you know what the hell I was talking about?"

The faceless man didn't answer for a moment. Then the darkness covering his face moved from side to side. "No," he admitted.

"And if I told you that where I come from, people are born, and they die, and when they die, they're buried, and their souls—"

"People are born here, too," the man cut in. "It happens all the time."

"And what do you mean by that? What does the word *born* mean to you?"

"It means what it means. It means they . . . arrive, they're here—"

"And where," David asked, "have they come from?"

Again the man didn't answer at once. He crossed the room, went to the bookcase, withdrew a particularly thick manuscript, opened it, and read:

"I saw a window, a room, a man. The man said, 'I love you, I love you.' Through the window a flat blue sky." The thin man paused. "I wrote this. So this, I believe, is where I come from. The place where there is a flat blue sky. It's not the sky we have here. We have a sky that moves and changes, as you've seen. I think that the place I came from, to be here, is a place of stillness."

David looked at the man for a long moment. Then he said, *"You* come from the same place that *I* came from."

In another city, a woman felt her way along narrow streets, her hand reaching for walls that were never close enough.

She needed walls.

She needed closeness.

And she needed space, too. She felt hungry for it. But she was fearful of that hunger. The out-of-doors was so numbing, so overwhelming, as if *it* were hungry for *her.*

The two needs—for closeness and for space—fought each other within her and at times she wept because she felt as if she were being pulled apart and compacted at the same time.

"Detective Kenner?" Karen Duffy said into Christian Grieg's telephone receiver, and told him who she was. She paused, then, uncertain how to continue.

"What can I help you with?" coaxed Leo Kenner.

She took a breath. "I'm a friend of David Case's. He's the brother of the woman who was murdered recently."

"Anne Case. Yes." His tone betrayed his piqued interest.

Again, Karen paused. She wasn't sure what she was doing, talking to the police. So what if Christian had had an affair with Anne Case. And so what if he had never told her, or David, about it. He was entitled to a private life. And his letters, and Anne's writings—on balance so ... bizarre. But no. That wasn't the right word. "I was simply wondering," she said to Leo Kenner, surprising herself by continuing the conversation, "how your investigation was proceeding."

"Actually," Kenner said, "there is no investigation, per se. We've pretty well established that . . ."

"Brian Fisher. Yes. I know." The words were coming out as if unbidden, now. "David told us."

"Us?"

"Yes. I have a friend. His name is Grieg. Perhaps you've heard of him—he's a writer—"

She hung up.

She kept her hand on the receiver. Her hand was shaking.

The woman in the yellow cottage on Sylvan Beach Road was there only for the day. She was making the cottage ready for her employers, who were planning on staying there for the weekend. Her employers had asked her to "freshen it," meaning that she should open all the windows and fluff up the pillows and air out the sheets and blankets—to generally dispel the clamminess that a closed-up lake cottage gathers to itself over the course of a winter and spring.

There had been no actual cleaning up to do. The cottage was as she had left it the previous autumn—spotless. The woman's employers had always insisted that it be that way, and she had always been only too happy to oblige. A dirty house—or even a house that wasn't spotless—was, after all, a reminder that, as she put it, "we're just one rung up from the animals." But, even though the cottage had been spotless, she had still cleaned it thoroughly, until it stank of lemon-scented spray cleaner, Lysol, and Spic'n'Span, a mixture of odors that—as she stood in the living room, her back to the front door—brought a broad smile to her pudgy, middle-aged face, a smile that said *God's in His heaven, all's right with the world.*

That smile froze when she heard a loud knock on the glass door behind her. She did not move for a moment, both surprised and a little fearful because the knock had been so loud, then she turned her head a quarter turn, so she could get some idea, at least, who was at the door. Out of the corner of her eye, she could see that it was probably a man. The figure at the door was stocky, mannish. She did not turn her head further for a moment. She didn't like the idea of a man being at the door while she was alone here. The neighbors had never been very friendly, and since none of the cottages nearby were yet in use for the summer, it was unlikely that the person at the door was a neighbor. So, by definition, it was a *strange man* at the door, and *strange man* easily translated, in her mind, as *dangerous man.*

Still, she realized, she had to be polite. She had to acknowledge the man—he could *see* her there, after all.

She turned, faced the door, studied the man in front of it for a moment, decided he looked harmless enough, except for the way his head was cocked, as if he were having a hard time seeing her, and except for his eyes, which seemed especially wide, somehow. And there was a queer sort of smile on his face—now that she thought about it. A crooked sort of smile, a Cheshire cat smile.

"What is it you want?" she said.

But the man did not reply. He continued to stare wide-eyed at her, continued to smile at her crookedly, his square head cocked.

"What is it you want?" she repeated, voice louder.

Still, he remained silent.

She quickly grew very afraid. People who stared

that way were people she did not want to be around. She was certainly not going to open the door for him. Should she move away from the door? she wondered. Go into the kitchen? To the second floor? What would *that* gain her?

She glanced quickly at the telephone on a small glass-and-wrought-iron end table nearby. She whispered a curse. The phone wasn't hooked up yet.

She looked back at the man at the door. She thought that he had shifted position a little. She wasn't sure. Yes, she realized. He *had* shifted position. He'd cocked his head the other way.

She felt her breathing grow quick, and shallow. She felt a sweat start under her arms.

This man, she realized, was a very dangerous man, and she did not have use of the phone, and running to another part of the little cottage would be stupid. It would gain her nothing. Only time.

She shouted at the man, "Get away!"

He did not move. He stayed silent.

"Get away!" she shouted again, and stepped quickly to the phone, visible from where the man was standing, picked it up, held the receiver to her ear, kept her eyes on the man all the while.

His lips moved. He'd said something, she realized. But she had heard nothing.

She kept the receiver to her ear. She planned to pretend to be talking to someone on it. She wondered frantically what words she would use. She didn't know. She had no idea. Dammit! Her fear was making her light-headed, stupid.

The man's lips moved again. Still she heard nothing.

She screamed at him, "What do you *want*?"

His lips moved again. Again soundlessly.

"Get away from here!" the woman screamed. "This is private property!"

She threw the phone down. She ran to the narrow stairway that led to the small upstairs bedroom. There was an access to the crawl-space attic there. That's where she'd hide.

She got halfway up the stairs when she heard the front door crash open.

In another part of Sylvan Beach, the small white dog that had gotten herself lost several days earlier was trying hard to get some sleep. It was very difficult. The dog had crawled under a porch, thinking she would be safe, but the darkness behind her was daunting, and every few moments she glanced around, certain that something was there, in the darkness—one of the dogs that had chased her, for instance.

The dog was so certain that something waited in the darkness behind her under the porch, in fact, that eventually she crawled out from under the porch, glanced anxiously about, and made her way through the bright sunlight, over the slippery rocks, to the beach.

FIFTEEN

Karen Duffy realized that she couldn't call Detective Kenner back. He'd think she was some kind of lunatic. Maybe he'd even think she knew something about Anne Case's murder.

Maybe she did know something about it. Maybe she knew quite a lot about it.

Wasn't that the reason she'd called Kenner in the first place?

She closed her eyes. Christ, yes, of course that was the reason.

She picked up the phone. Put it down. Picked it up again.

"Fred," Detective Kenner said to Fred Collins over the phone, "did you interview someone named Karen Duffy in connection with the Anne Case homicide?"

"No," Collins answered. He was at home. He was very tired. "I don't think so. Why?"

Kenner told him about Karen's phone call, then said he had tried to call her at home but there had been no answer.

"Maybe she wasn't calling from home," Collins suggested.

"Or maybe she wasn't answering the phone," Kenner said.

"Are you going to pursue it further?" Collins asked.

"Yes," Kenner answered.

The rest of the yellow cottage was spotless, but the crawl-space attic was home to a hundred varieties of spiders and insects; the cellulose insulation—installed two decades earlier—had begun to disintegrate and, because there was an opening to the crawl space from under the eaves—caused by the effects of dry rot—the brisk winds that day pushed the distintegrating insulation about like dust.

The pudgy-faced housekeeper hiding in the crawl space—she was hunched precariously on the joists; there was no floor, only the old, rotting joists, the decaying insulation between, the Sheetrock kitchen ceiling below—could see nothing except a sliver of yellowish light at the bottom of the small attic-access door. But she could feel a hundred tiny legs tickling her exposed arms and calves, and the cellulose dust blowing about was quickly clogging her nose so she had to breathe through her mouth, which was nearly impossible because her terror was forcing her to breathe very rapidly. As a consequence, she was hyperventilating and becoming dizzy.

She did not think it was possible she was going to die.

She thought it was a certainty.

She began to pray. Silently.

And somewhere behind her terror, she wondered about heaven.

"David?" Christian Grieg mouthed silently. "David? I know you're up here." No words came out, only the passage of air, a whisper so small even he could not have heard it.

The small room stank of cleaning fluids. This displeased him. David was trying to clean him out of his life. That wasn't friendly. They had known each other a good long time—Who knew how long?—and now David wanted to clean him out of his life, as if he—Christian—were nothing more than a spot of dirt, a mote of dust, a stain.

"David?" he mouthed. "David?" He looked about. A full-sized bed, beige comforter, newly fluffed pillows. A nightstand—oak. A wastebasket. Track lighting above. "David, I saw you come up here." No words. Only air. He moved quietly across the room, to the front of the bed. He looked right. A window. It opened onto the lake. There were whitecaps. They were silent. The room was silent. "David?" Air moving. "David?" He looked left. The door. The stairs. A chest of drawers. Cherry. A mirror.

A man was there, in the mirror. He stood silently, eyes wide, head cocked, mouth crooked.

"Hello," Christian said.

"Hello," said the man in the mirror.

Christian looked straight ahead. Another door. Much shorter, waist-high. Closet? he wondered. Attic?

"David?" Only air. Stillness. Silence.

He leaned over. There was no knob, just a rectangular block of wood nailed vertically to the door. He grasped the block of wood, pulled it. The door would not open.

He chuckled silently.

He pulled the door harder.

He heard a scream from beyond the door, the sound of wood cracking, another scream, something thumping hard—with grim finality—to the kitchen floor below.

"David," he said.

The woman stretched her arms out to touch the walls that were never close enough. She needed closeness. She needed space. She felt pulled and compacted all at once. She wept. She laughed.

She remembered.

The soft oval face of a man with sensitive gray eyes.

"Brian," the woman said. But it meant nothing to her. It was a little more than a tic, a random movement of her lips, that made her feel warm for an instant.

Then the face dissipated.

And, again, the woman found herself trying almost desperately' to reach the walls that were never close enough.

The thin man sat in an uncomfortable-looking wooden rocking chair and sipped orange pekoe tea from a delicate blue teacup as he rocked. White daylight streaming in through the room's tall, narrow window illuminated his legs, his middle, his legs, his middle.

He has been watching David for some time.

Because David, standing very still near the manuscript-laden bookcase, had not spoken for some time.

The faceless man wanted to coax David. He wanted to ask David lots of questions—questions that had plagued the man forever, questions the man was certain David could answer. But the man was telling himself that he had patience and sensitivity, and that he knew that David had suddenly become very troubled. So, he would hold his tongue for the moment. It was difficult—his lips quivered with the effort—but he remained silent.

Suddenly the light through the room's one window grew dimmer. "Darkness again," the man said, and wanted desperately to elaborate.

David said nothing.

"It's very unusual," the man said. "Darkness so soon after darkness."

"Darkness," David whispered. "My sister's name is Anne."

"Anne," said the faceless man wonderingly.

"She's here. Anne's here," David said, and his voice rose in pitch as he spoke, as the excitement and certainty mounted within him. "Anne is here. In this city. I can *feel* it!"

"Anne," the thin man whispered, lost in the name, trying to find meaning in it. He said, "Sister," and wondered at it. He said, "Anne," and wondered at it. "Anne. Sister," he said.

"I can't stay here," David said, and started for the door.

The faceless man rose abruptly from his chair, sending it rocking way back, until it nearly fell, then way forward. The faceless man crossed the room in a moment. He grabbed David's arm.

David looked at the man's long, dark fingers, then into the man's face, the large eyes, wide nose. The mouth was set in a stern, straight line.

The man said, "I can see your face now. I think that that may be of some significance.

Christian stared silently at the chunky woman lying dead on the kitchen floor of the yellow cottage. The woman was on her back, her arms wide, ankles crossed beneath her calf-length blue house-dress. The dress had ridden up to just above her fat, dimpled white knees.

She was surrounded and covered by bits of gray cellulose insulation, whitish-gray Sheetrock and blond lengths of splintered, decayed, floor joists. Spiders of varying sizes and colors—they had fallen with her from the attic crawl-space—were busily retreating to hiding places in the kitchen.

The woman's eyes were open and Christian thought that that was interesting—whatever could she be looking at?

"Well, now," he said aloud, and leaned over and put his open hand on the woman's face, so his palm was on her nose, and his lower palm was on her mouth, and his fingers were touching her open eyes. He had never touched the open eyes of another person. He had always been interested in how they might feel. Moist? Cool? Warm? He found that the chunky woman's eyes were cool and hard, like whole eggs.

He lingered with his open hand on her face for half a minute, then he straightened and gently toed her at the waist. He whispered at her, "Dead, huh?"

He sighed. He had the wrong cottage, that was obvious. But the past few minutes here had been wonderfully entertaining.

"Detective Kenner, this is Karen Duffy again. I'm afraid we . . . somehow we got cut off a few minutes ago. It's this phone, I think. It's very old. One of those black table models that weighs a ton—"

"Could you tell me where you're calling from, Miss Duffy?" Kenner interrupted.

"Do you mean you want the number here? The

telephone number?" She started to give him the number.

He interrupted again, "No. Whose house are you calling from? Your own?"

A moment's silence. Then, "Christian's house," she said.

"That's the man you mentioned earlier? The writer?"

"Yes. Christian Grieg."

"Could you spell that, please."

"Grieg? Of course." She spelled it. "And Christian, his first name, is spelled as you'd imagine it is."

Kenner spelled Christian for her, anyway, then asked, "Is that right?"

"That's right, yes," she answered, her voice shaky.

"Are you nervous, Miss Duffy?"

She hesitated, then said, "A little, certainly." She was trying to sound casual, offhand. "I imagine that lots of people are nervous talking to police detectives."

"Of course. Could you tell me the reason for your call, please?"

Silence.

"Miss Duffy?"

"I'm not sure." Her voice still was shaky. "Perhaps I've . . ." Silence.

"Please, Miss Duffy."

"No, I'm sorry for bothering you unnecessarily," she said. Then there was a click, a dial tone.

"Goddammit!" Kenner whispered. He got the phone book out of his desk drawer and looked up Christian Grieg's number and address.

"Ah, but there you go again," said the thin man. "I can't see you." He sounded playful. "It's sort of a game of peekaboo you're playing, isn't it?"

"No," David said, his tone heavy with meaning. "No game. I'm dying."

The thin man shook his head; the darkness covering his face moved from side to side.

"You haven't the faintest idea what I'm talking about, do you?" David said.

"I don't know about dying," the man said. "God, I don't know about dying, but I surely want to, I have *always* wanted to know about dying, ever since I first put the word to paper—"

There was a loud, harsh gurgling noise from close by.

The man crossed quickly to a length of fat gray pipe that emerged from the floor near the darkened window and disappeared into the ceiling. He rapped on the pipe. The gurgling stopped. "Unequal pressure," he said. "No one knows why. There are these pipes everywhere. They go down through the houses and then into the ground, and from time to time they make that awful noise."

David turned toward the open door and the darkness. He said, "I know that my sister Anne is out there, in the city somewhere. I can *feel* it. That's why I have to leave." He felt very odd, suddenly. Light-headed and heavy and bloated all at once, as if he had eaten too much and drunk too much and was just beginning to feel the effects.

"Then leave," said the thin man.

David looked back at him. The darkness covering the man's face dissipated all at once, as if it were merely an exhale on a cold day, and David saw the man's wide nose, and large, friendly eyes, and full mouth. There was a look of bemusement on it. "Leave?" David said.

The man said nothing.

"Go into the darkness?" David was astonished by the idea.

Still the man said nothing.

"Who goes willingly into the darkness?"

"No one," the man said, and reached and closed the door. "Some orange pekoe tea, then?"

"Tea?" David said.

"Orange pekoe."

"Yes," David said.

SIXTEEN

Leo Kenner knocked for the third time on Christian Grieg's front door and, receiving no answer, put his hand to the knob and tried it. The door was unlocked. He opened it, stuck his head in through the opening.

"Hello?" he called, and looked about, past the small foyer, into the large, neat living room. "Is anyone here? Mr. Grieg? Miss Duffy?" He listened. The house was silent. The driveway had been empty. No one was at home, that was obvious.

White house, green shutters, green house, white shutters. White shutters, white shutters . . .

"David, dammit, David—"

Christian's foot lost purchase on a slick beach rock and he almost toppled backwards. But he made his arms flail about as if he were a windmill, let out a couple of enthusiastic "Whoops!" and stayed upright, barely.

"Oh, I do feel *very* foolish!" he whispered. "Foolish, foolish, oh foolish me!"

A gull, intent on a fish carcass, screeched at him from nearby. Three gulls had found the fish carcass. One gull stretched its neck out and flat-footed it after another, who ran squawking away. Then the aggressive gull put its attention once more on Christian, and screeched again. Christian screeched back. The gull stared for a moment, beak shut tight, dark eyes full of confusion.

Christian, who was not very far off, put his arms out, as if he were a bird, lowered his head, and ran at the three gulls, scaring them away from the fish carcass. They flew squawking into the air. One—the easily bullied—went off toward land and the other two went off over the water, where they circled at a good stone's-throw distance and watched him uneasily, certain he was going to steal their fish.

But he brought his foot down very hard on it, instead, and mashed it into a gray, bony, pulpy mass on the beach stones. This pleased him.

After a moment, he continued his search for David.

The woman asked herself, *How large is this place?* but she was uncertain of the significance of the question, or of how it pertained to her.

She remembered coming here.

She remembered the house. The windows free of glass. The open doorways. That was the starting point. The beginning. (And how was that significant? Beginning? What did it mean?)

She remembered leaving the house.

Remembered the forest.

People gathered around.

But these memories were fading quickly, as a dream does.

And now there was this city, these houses and brick streets. The smells of cooking and of animals—a heady mixture. *Life goes on here!* she thought, and was momentarily happy because of it, though she did not know why. *Life?* she wondered.

A shadow approached. It darkened the brick street, the close wooden walls of the houses. Then it passed over her and made her shiver.

She turned, looked where it had gone. She saw it receding, darkening the streets and houses as it went. She looked up, thought something had flown over; there was nothing visible in the slim rectangular path between the houses, only the fiercely moving white and gray and blue sky.

This word escaped her: "Christian." She heard it, wondered briefly at it, and, like the shadow on the brick streets and wooden walls, it made her momentarily cold.

Then it too was gone, and she forgot it.

Christian saw at last the green cottage with white shutters and he stared at it for a long time, while the gulls screeched their complaints at him from above for his destruction of their meal.

But he paid them no attention.

He kept his attention on the cottage. On its lines and its green-ness. He though that it was very green—a lovely, deep green reminiscent of grass that has been allowed to grow tall and thick.

Above and out over the lake, the gulls screeched one last complaint in unison and then flew off.

He paid them no attention.

He did not become aware of the sudden quiet.

Because his mind was not quiet.

There was the sound of wind in it, a wind blowing the lovely, thick grass which rustled and swished and made a noise like water crashing over rocks.

Wind and water.

"David!" he yelled. And could not hear himself over the white noise, in his head, of the wind and the water.

He yelled "David!" again, and again.

Then he stopped.

The wind and water stopped.

Blessed silence.

Deep, blessed silence.

No sound.

His mouth moved. Air. His friend's name moving on the air. *David.*

David.

David.

Slow movements of air, a little whisper, the whisper of sleep, the sound of dying.

He moved forward, toward the green cottage.

BOOK THREE

IS, WAS, AND IS

ONE

I t is ten years later. Maude and Peter, who live in the house that once belonged to Anne Case, have invited a half dozen friends over. Some of these friends are people that Maude and Peter have known for some time; some are new friends, or lovers, of Maude and Peter's old friends. A formal dinner of veal parmigiana, stuffed grape leaves, and chocolate mousse has been enjoyed, and people are wandering about with cups of coffee or espresso in hand, when Maude suggests that they hold a séance to try and contact the spirit of Anne Case, which, Maude explains, she's seen moving "with great sadness" from room to room. "Mostly upstairs, you know. In that huge room on the third floor. I see her there quite a lot, in fact." It's a gentle lie. It's meant only to heighten the atmosphere of romantic moodiness that Maude feels pervades the house, anyway.

"Really?" says a young, svelte, dark-haired woman named Barbara; she's clearly incredulous but intrigued.

"How terribly bizarre," says another woman, also young and also svelte.

"Well, yes, it is bizarre," Maude says. "But she *was* murdered, after all, and, as you know, such a dark death precludes any possibility of rest or peace at all."

"Poor thing," Barbara mutters.

"Precisely," Maude agrees, and repeats her interest in holding a séance to try and contact the spirit of Anne Case.

There are a few reservations about the idea of a séance, but there is much more in the way of enthusiasm, so the people in the house busy themselves with arranging the heavy, wooden, kitchen chairs in a circle, which is the way—they know after watching dozens of movies and endless hours of TV—that all good séances are prepared.

"Anyone for more mousse?" asks Maude.

"Is there more?" a man asks enthusiastically.

"Is there?" Maude asks Peter.

"I'll check," Peter says, and goes into the kitchen. He comes back a few moments later, looking crestfallen. "No more mousse, I'm afraid."

"No mousse, I'm afraid," Maude declares. "So I guess we can get started."

There are some grumblings of disappointment, then the lights are dimmed and nearly everyone takes a seat.

There's a minute of self-conscious babble, some giggling; a man, still standing, protests that "this is nothing to fool around with, you know," but he quickly makes himself part of the circle, too.

Then, very solemnly, Maude bids them all to join hands.

They do it.

There's another giggle.

Barbara says, "Boo!"

The séance begins.

TWO

I n his quick search of Christian's house, Leo
Kenner found nothing but a half-completed
letter from Christian to someone unknown—
there was no salutation—which spoke of "urgen-
cies" and "desperations," and ended up giving Leo
the very odd feeling that he'd met this man—
Christian Grieg—before, though he was positive
he hadn't.

He folded the letter—one handwritten page that
he'd found under a coffee table in the living
room—put it in his sportscoat pocket, and quickly
left the house.

David asked the thin man if he had ever heard
of the phenomenon of interior voices. The man
said that he hadn't, and David told him about various murderers he had read about—"The Son of
Sam, for instance," he said—who had been moved
in their actions by interior voices. These people

were certain that the voices they heard were, indeed, not interior at all, that they were real people—or, in the case of the Son of Sam, real animals—who had the right and the power to tell them what to do, and most often what they told people like the Son of Sam to do was to kill other people.

The thin man said that he did not understand, because he didn't know what "kill" meant, but that he very much wanted to understand, and David told him that he, David—he did not name himself; he could no longer name himself, although his memory was replete with the names of others—was beginning to hear interior voices and these voices were telling him to get away, to go back down the tunnel, back to the earth before it was too late.

To which the thin man said, "What tunnel? What earth?"

And David, though he tried mightily to answer him, had no answer.

So he began to weep, and to feel very alone, and very afraid.

Karen Duffy said, "Well then, where *is* Detective Kenner?"

The desk sergeant said, "I'm sorry, I can't give you that information."

"Shit!" Karen breathed.

"He'll be back shortly," the desk sergeant said, and nodded at a couple of brown metal folding chairs set up near the double front doors. "Why don't you wait for him."

"I *can't* wait," Karen told him. "Don't you understand, if I wait . . . if I wait, then—"

"You could speak to another detective," the desk sergeant suggested, sensing a strange sort of urgency in Karen's tone. "Why don't you do that, Miss . . . Miss . . . "

Karen turned suddenly, whispered "Dammit to hell!" and left the building.

Christian was remembering Anne Case's last moment, and he was finding some glee in it, like a high school basketball star remembering the best shot of his career.

Christian could see the point of his small knife going in through Anne's gray housedress, and in his mind's eye he could see the point of the knife puncturing her heart, and her heart deflating slowly.

It had maddened him, then. It had made him do the thing he would never have thought of doing otherwise, the thing he remembered so often, the thing which was, now, only a blur of movement, quick and abstract, like the beating of a hummingbird's wings. The knife coming up, the knife going down, the knife going in, and the knife coming up, the knife going down, the knife going in, and the knife coming up, the knife going down, the knife—

It replayed over and again in his head, like a song. He could *hear* it—the passage of air, the movement of his arm through the air. *Whoosh!* It *was* song. *Whoosh, thump!* . . . *Whoosh, thump!* So beautiful!

So beautiful!

Whoosh, thump, whoosh thump. Whoosh. Thump! Thump!

He pushed open the front door of the green cottage and told David, whom he could not yet see, "I love you, my friend."

In Anne Case's house, the martins had fled through an open window on the third floor, and the spiders and insects that had been their food were again insinuating themselves in the house's many rooms.

"I don't remember coming here," David said. "I think I should remember coming here."

He was confused, astonished, frightened. He felt alone, and afraid, like a child who comes home to an empty house for the first time in his life and tries to convince himself that he's actually in someone else's house. But it *is* his house, the child knows. And it's a very strange place, now, because no one else is in it; it echoes appallingly, and the rooms are too large, or too small, and the shadows cast by lamps and chairs and tables are shadows the child does not remember seeing in the house before.

The thin man said enthusiastically, "Tell me about dying. I want to know about dying." His face vanished into darkness, returned, vanished. "It sounds intriguing; it sounds like some experience I would like to have—though I really can't say how I would know that—"

"I don't know about dying," David told him.

"I'm disappointed," said the faceless man simply.

David looked at the window. "I know about darkness," he whispered.

"Everyone knows about darkness," said the faceless man. "When it comes, some people stay away from it, and some people don't. Some people welcome it. But when they welcome it, no one sees them again. And no one knows where they've gone off to, either." He paused. "It's a very wonderful mystery."

The green cottage smelled of lake air.

THREE

The body lay on its back halfway into the green cottage through the side door.

"Lilac perfume," said the elderly man to the deputy sheriff. "That's what you're smelling."

The deputy leaned back from the open driver's window of the shiny blue Toyota. He said grimly, "It looks like someone made her drink it, then strangled her."

The woman with the crown of black hair lay very still. A couple of flies buzzed about inside the Toyota. One settled on the woman's cheek; the deputy, seeing this, grimaced and said, "Jesus, flies."

The elderly man said, "That's a very perverse thing for someone to do, Deputy—making that woman drink her own perfume. A man who would do something like that would have to have a very dark soul."

"Yes, sir," the deputy said. "Very dark indeed."

Another patrol car pulled up then, lights flashing.

Christian was on his haunches near the green cottage's side door; his knees were close to David's face; David's mouth was open a little, and his eyes were closed lightly, as if he were asleep. Christian was running his fingers through David's hair.

"Are you already dead, my friend?" Christian mouthed. No sound came out. Only air. "Dead already, David?"

But he thought not.

It did not seem so.

David's chest wasn't moving, but his skin was warm. He was in some twilight sleep, clearly.

I'm going to have to kill you myself, aren't I? Christian mouthed. He felt so pleased and titillated by the idea that a rush of excitement coursed through him and made him tremble.

He took his hand away from David's hair. His fingers were damp and trembling; David's hair was wet, he realized.

He cocked his head at this. Before dancing off to the other side, David had made sure that his hair was clean and fresh.

Christian stayed on his haunches. *Before his death, the man washed his hair.*

He watched as his fingers continued to tremble. Finally, they quieted.

How am I going to kill you, my friend?

The method was so important. Method in life was everything everything.

He would have to do it with finesse. And with subtlety.

Just as he had with Anne.

And with the woman in the blue Toyota. Making her strangle on her own perfume.

He couldn't simply drop a very large rock on David's head. It would get the job done, certainly, but it wouldn't get it done with the care and artistry that the task demanded. It would be brutish to drop a rock on his head.

Too large a rock would leave David disfigured and unrecognizable. If, in the instant before the rock went *Sploosh!* onto his head, David awakened from his gentle twilight sleep and saw what was happening, and he got a look on his face of great revelation and astonishment, that look would be lost forever. His lips and teeth would be squashed this way and that, and his nose would be flattened, and his eyes—depending on the jaggedness of the particular rock that was used—might well puncture. And punctured eyes were wholly incapable of expression. So, no one anywhere would talk about the look on David's face when he died, because he would have no face. The people who discovered David's body would never say, "He looked astonished. Did you see?"

It *would* be possible, on the other hand, to drop a rock on David's throat and crush his windpipe. That would lead to suffocation. Such an act would leave no marks at all on David's face. David's face might well bear an expression of revelation and astonishment, and so people would talk about it for a long time.

Oh, these were dark, dark thoughts, weren't they, on such a fair and breezy afternoon.

(But he had always been fond of darkness.)

Or he could get a pillow and do it

or simply put his hand over David's nose and mouth or get a knife a big knife from the kitchen and push it all the way into David's chest

* * *

"About an hour, I think," the first deputy said to the deputy who had just joined him. "Judging from body temperature, I'd say an hour."

The other deputy—older, jaded—smiled to himself, went over to the Toyota, leaned into the window, sniffed, and said, "Jesus, what's that smell?"

"Lilac perfume," the other deputy told him.

"Yes," said the elderly man.

"Is it?" said the second deputy. "It's awful."

"Well, sure," said the first deputy, "but I think you're putting that smell into the context of the event—"

The second deputy looked around at him. "Huh?"

The first deputy shrugged. "Nothing. Just talking. Do you think I should try and go find someone who might know this woman?"

"You haven't looked at her driver's license?"

"Not yet. I thought I should leave everything alone."

The second deputy sighed. "Sure. You were probably right to do that. But you could have called the plate number into DMV." He straightened. "I'll do that. You go and see if you can find someone who might have seen something here. This area's mostly deserted this time of year, so I doubt you'll have much luck." He paused. "I'll radio you with this woman's ID."

"Uhdarcknass," wrote the chunky man in the below-ground-level apartment, "like knowuthar chasez hymn awl over thuh plas—and he looks bahk and ittz ganeingon hymn fasst, he's knott wonteeng 2b quik enuf oar he wants it to catch hymn, this theeng frum insid hymn—"

FOUR

It is ten years later. People are gathered for a séance in what was once Anne Case's house.

They're clasping hands in a circle while the lights are dim.

Some of them have shut their eyes.

Some are looking about in the semidarkness, at the others, and wondering, variously, if this is a proper way for adults to spend their time; if the ones who have their eyes closed are sleeping, or if they really believe this stuff; if the woman of the house really thinks that the ghost of Anne Case still walks here.

And perhaps she does, some of them think.

Maude is the one who's expected to lead this séance, but she's temporarily at a loss because she has never led a séance before and isn't certain of the protocol. It would be terrible, she thinks, to offend the spirits of those departed with the wrong terms or salutations. It would be even more terrible to offend the spirit of Anne Case or, and the thought is very fleeting, the stocky, mannish thing that she has seen in the house.

Does anyone know how to begin? Maude wants to ask. And she almost asks it, but, not wanting to appear foolish, begins instead, "We are gathered in this circle, Anne, to appeal to you to . . . to speak to us, to show us a sign. For ten years you have been silent. Now you may speak."

It's a good beginning, she believes.

She continues, "I have seen you here, Anne, and I know of your loneliness—"

There's a giggle from somewhere in the circle and Maude hesitates, looks around the circle stonily for the giggler, says, "I know this *seems* funny to most of you"—she hopes that she doesn't sound too terribly severe— "and if I were in your shoes, I'd be giggling, too, I'm sure. But just imagine what can be accomplished here if we simply focus all of our . . . uh . . . spiritual energy on this for a few minutes."

"Sorry," Barbara says from across the circle. "I'm a little nervous about this whole thing, I guess."

Maude says, "It's okay. We're only human, after all." She hesitates, takes a breath, goes on, "Let's start over again, shall we."

In a far corner of the house, something stirs, and awakes. It has been trapped in the house for nearly a decade, and it is tinglingly aware of a kinship between itself and the gathering of souls in the house. The love of darkness that they share.

FIVE

The view David had out the room's tall window was of a wooden building across the narrow street; the street itself, made of brick; and, if he leaned out the window, and looked up, a long, rectangular slice of the furiously moving gray and blue sky.

The building across the street—it seemed only an arm's length away, though that was probably an illusion; it was probably twenty feet or more from the window he was looking out of—was decorated with drawings done in what could have been charcoal, and with what looked like colorful oil paints—deep red, bright yellow, a strange, phosphorescent blue. Some of the drawings seemed to have actually been carved into the wood.

The drawings were everywhere. They snaked across the tops of windows, connected windows and doors. And they depicted many things. There were what looked like people. There were animals, buildings, mountains, trees.

Many of the drawings were childlike—some of the people were mere stick figures, some of the mountains simple triangular shapes, and the trees like straws with a ball at one end.

But many of the drawings were wonderfully rendered, by artists who were obviously possessed of great talent.

"Do people get on ladders to do those drawings?" David asked.

The thin man rose from the chair he'd been sitting in and joined David at the window. "Yes, I've seen them do that from time to time. I've never done it myself, of course. I don't believe that I'm so inclined. But the people who do it seem very happy. They smile. They laugh. They seem as happy as they can be, as happy as clams, I think, and seeing them doing these things, these things that make them happy, I feel very happy for them—"

David looked at the man's face as the man talked. The man's eyes were large, brown; they glistened, as if the man had been weeping, though David had not seen him weeping, and his mouth was heavy-lipped, the nose wide and flat.

David said, interrupting the man's monologue, "I don't believe that I've always been able to see your face the way I'm seeing it now."

"Nor I yours," the man said.

Christian Grieg thought, *The Benefits of Suffocation by Pillow:*

The primal, desperate, stiff gesticulations of a body experiencing oxygen starvation.

The quick and muffled noises of confusion and mortal frustration.

The irony of one strong man killing another with goose down.

The possibility that the victim will pee his pants.

And afterward, a last expression—frozen between life and death—of frothy horror and disbelief.

The deputy sheriff had seen no cars parked at the cottages at this end of Sylvan Beach and he believed that the older deputy had been right; the beach was probably all but deserted at this time of year, so the chances that anyone had seen anything were remote, at best.

He radioed to the older deputy that he had found nothing, that he would now be checking the east section of the beach, made a quick K-turn, and started back the way he had come.

Moments later, the older deputy radioed the name of the murdered woman. "Last name Pierce, first name Violet," he said, and the younger deputy wondered if Violet Pierce had any relatives who would have to be notified. Of course she did, he thought. Everyone had relatives somewhere. *(I'm sorry, I have bad news; your wife—aunt, mother, grandmother, girlfriend, confidante—was murdered by a person or persons unknown. Before her death, she had the contents of a one-fluid-ounce jar of lilac perfume poured into her mouth.)*

He brought his car to a quick stop on the road. There was a garage attached to the little green cottage he was looking at; the garage door was closed. The deputy wondered about this. There were no windows in the garage door. Perhaps there was a car inside.

In the room, there were big, sturdy wooden chairs, and wide, overstuffed couches that nobody ever sat in; there was an empty bookcase, and a floor lamp minus a cord and switch. There were paintings on the wall, too—each a simple wedding of color and line, like an Easter parade seen through dust.

The room opened onto half a dozen other rooms similarly furnished. There were no doors between the rooms, and no doors at all in the house, not even in the entranceway, or in the back, where the kitchen led out to a thousand acres of clover. There were openings for doors, but no doors.

There were openings for windows, but no glass.

The house was like many others. It was the way houses were built here, as if planned from a memory that was incomplete.

People came and went from these houses, but no one claimed ownership of them and no one spent any time in them.

That was the way things were here, too.

The house was made of pine and green clapboard put together with common nails. It had two stories and an attic, a front porch, a back porch, and a cellar.

The creatures that lived in the cellar might, at a quick glance, have been mistaken for creatures that lived in many cellars. They burrowed into wood and dug holes in the ground. They made noises at night. And if the light was right, their eyes shone. They were creatures of the darkness, and they were as old as humankind. People had created them and people sustained them.

On occasion, rain came to the area where the house had been built. It pelted the stone tile roof, cascaded over the edge to the ground, soaked in, and was gone. Evaporation did not exist here.

Sometimes, people danced in the house and around it.

The people had no names. In this place no one did.

Darkness came.

The creatures that lived in the cellar of the house moved gracefully, like water, up the stairs and across the floors, through the doorways and over the windowsills, out into the fields of clover.

Nothing moved in these fields. So the things returned to the cellar.

Light came.

A barely perceptible groan escaped the body lying half in the doorway to the green cottage.

Christian Grieg, standing nearby, goose-down pillow in a blue striped pillowcase in hand, heard it and smiled. "Well now, Davey boy," he said. "Alive, alive-o."

It pleased him immensely that David was alive.

His fingers trembled.

He got down on his haunches, put his hand to David's chest. There was no movement, no life. Only warmth.

He heard a car pull away on the road seventy-five feet north. He dimly noted the car's passage, as if it were no more than a fly buzzing in another part of the room. He looked up briefly from his friend lying still. He saw dust rising in the dry, breezy, sunlit air above the unpaved road.

He focused again on David, on his own trembling fingers on David's chest.

He thought that he had always liked his own fingers. He thought that they were artistic.

Perhaps it would be better indeed to bring peace to his friend with his fingers, his thumbs pressed hard to David's windpipe, which was, he felt certain, the way such murders were carried out.

He glanced up again at the unpaved road seventy-five feet north. The dust was beginning to settle. It was no longer sunlit. A bank of clouds had come over.

Christian smiled.

He tossed the pillow aside.

He would bring darkness to David with his very own fingers, which is the way such things should always be between friends.

Personal.

And affectionate.

SIX

It is ten years later.

Something stirs in the house that once belonged to Anne Case, but no one gathered below for an impromptu séance is aware of it.

"We *know* of your presence here!" Maude declares loudly, feeling a little self-conscious about the volume of her voice and its pitch, close to a shriek.

Some of the others gathered in the circle glance at her and smile, then look back down again, and close their eyes. They have never seen Maude act this way before, and while it amuses them, it also leads them to think that she may be onto something. Perhaps there really is an entity (ghost, spirit, wraith, whatever) that walks the house, and speaks to her, and wants an end to loneliness.

It isn't so hard to believe.

It is, after all, only what any creature wants. An end to loneliness.

While, above them, something has stirred and awakened and has begun to move through the space of the house toward the people gathered below.

It is a creature that knows nothing of time, but everything of pain. And loneliness.

It is a creature that craves the dark.

David thought, *All of this is an illusion. None of it exists. These are dreams. I am still connected to the earth, and what I'm seeing here are only a dying man's interpretations of earthly things.*

Just as when his mind had transformed the small fish that swam in the shallows of Oneida Lake into swiftly moving insects, biting mosquitoes into foraging honeybees, and the earth itself—the lake he'd been walking in; the cottages that lined it—into a ghost of itself. (Just as he had told himself, too, that he was wearing corduroy pants, white shirt, shoes. He was wearing nothing; nor was he naked. He formed for himself the image of his hands as he moved, the right and left inward curves of his shoes as he moved. He conjured up the sounds of his feet trudging over the floor. But there was no sound except the whispers of his past.)

So now, as well, he was dreaming.

The thin and annoyingly talkative man with him here was a character in the dream.

The window he—David—stood at was a fixture in the dream, and so was the building across the street and its intricate and colorful drawings, the brick streets, the furiously moving sky.

All of it was a dream. No more than a dream.

A face came to him. It was oval, pretty, smiling. It was framed by dark wood. (*These snapshots were nothing more than animal protein and a cou-*

*ple layers of dye and silver nitrate that the light
got at for a microsecond.)*

"Anne?" he said. "My God, what am I *doing*
here?"

The thin man touched David's hand, which was
on the windowsill.

David looked up from the man's hand to his
face. It was lost in darkness.

Words came from the darkness. "I think that
you must go back to wherever you came from. I
think that you can stay here no longer."

The deputy pulled in behind Christian's Buick,
which was parked fifty feet down a narrow dead-
end path bordered on both sides by cattails, radioed in the car's license number, and was told,
after a few moments, that there were no "wants
or warrants" for the car's registered owner.

The deputy hesitated, ready to back out onto
Sylvan Beach Road.

After a couple of seconds, he shut the patrol car
off, closed the door, and approached the Buick
cautiously, one hand on the strap that held his
service revolver in its holster.

He unstrapped the revolver, put his hand on the
grip. He barked, "Is there anyone in the car?"

The cattails around him danced in a sudden
brisk wind.

The deputy pursed his lips. He was a little
scared, and he knew precisely why—the murder
of Violet Pierce; this car abandoned here, on this
narrow, dead-end path that was bordered by tall
cattails.

The quiet.

Of course he was scared.

He drew his service revolver, pointed it straight
up. "You in the car!" he barked. "Out. Now!"

But he could see no one in the car, and he suddenly felt foolish as well as scared.

Around him, the cattails danced.

"Dammit!" he whispered.

Distantly, from somewhere on the lake, he heard the ragged hum of an outboard motor.

Christian Grieg thought, *All these things are foolish.*

Pillows.

Goose down. Big rocks and thumbs
Thumbs
such foolish things.

The watchword was affection. David was his friend. He loved David. He had always loved David.

David was deserving of his affection and his gentle touch and caress and he had

himself breathed life into David not too long ago and not too far from this very spot either

breathed life into him so why not

WHY NOT

SUCK IT OUT OF HIM, the very air, the air that pumped his lungs up and kept him in this twilight sleep WHY NOT

lay down beside him there with affection and pinch his nose shut and do that same thing he had done before only

IN REVERSE,

SUCK OUT THE LIFE, SUCK OUT THE LIFE

The woman crouched in a doorway and looked up at the slice of moving sky high overhead. She felt alone, it was true. She felt hemmed in, it was true. She felt the need for space, and the need for closeness, and the two needs fought themselves within her and made her insides knot up. It was true.

But she did not feel pain.

And she remembered pain. It was like a tug from behind that was designed to keep her from moving forward.

She felt a little dizzy, even as she crouched in the doorway. But then she stood, shakily, the word "Brian" escaped her, and was gone, and forgotten.

A shadow moved swiftly at a distance down the narrow brick street. It darkened the houses as it made its way toward her. But when she looked up, thinking that something must be flying over, a bird, perhaps, something very large, she saw nothing. And when she looked back, down the narrow street and the close-packed houses, she saw nothing. The shadow had gone.

"Christian," she said, and then the name was gone, too.

She was bathed in light.

And her memory of pain began to fade.

"Uhdarcknass," wrote the chunky man in the below-ground-level apartment, "like knowuthar chasez hymn awl over thuh plas—and he looks bahk and ittz ganeingon hymn fasst, he's knott wonteeng 2b quik enuf oar he wants it to catch hymn, this theeng frum insid hymn. it chaases lika dawg awoolf, a murdereeng theeng and it wonts2 overwelm hymn, eet hymn, mak hymn itself"

SEVEN

It is ten years later.

The people gathered in what was once Anne Case's house are of various minds about what they're doing, sitting in a circle, listening to—making themselves a part of—entreaties being made to the dead to appear, to show themselves.

One woman thinks mostly of her son, and the tough time he's having in school. She's worried about his future. She thinks that he may end up in a dead-end job and be unhappy for the rest of his life because he will always have to worry about money. Her thoughts are only partially with what Maude is doing. She thinks that it's a bit silly.

Another woman is frightened. She believes that there are things moving in the house and that they intend harm to them all, and that Maude is being foolhardy indeed playing with the supernatural in this way.

"*Speak* to us, show us a *sign*, Anne!" Maude pleads.

And the thing in another part of the house that has stirred and awakened has made its way to the top of the stairs, and has started down.

In the semidarkness below, a man gathered with the others in a circle for the séance looks toward the stairs, and his head cocks a little because he thinks he's heard something. After a moment, he looks away. A shiver goes through him.

"I have *seen* you here, Anne!" Maude declares.

"I'm sorry," says a young man—youngest in this group made of mostly of thirty-to-forty-year-olds. His name is Dorian. "But I really have to use the bathroom. Do you mind?"

Maude gives him an oblique, subtly offended look. Then she says, "Upstairs. Second door on the right."

Dorian stands, smiles quiveringly. He is very embarrassed. "It's okay," he says, and sweeps his hand to include the circle remaining, "go ahead without me."

"We can wait," Maude says.

"I won't be long, then," says Dorian, and starts for the stairs.

When the deputy stood beside the open driver's window of the Buick that was parked down the dead-end path off Sylvan Beach Road, he smelled lilacs.

Lilacs? he wondered.

There were no lilac bushes here. Only cattails moving fitfully in what had, in the past few moments, become a stiff breeze.

Lilacs?

He leaned into the driver's window.

Lilacs?

He saw that the keys were in the ignition.

Lilacs? he wondered. *Lilac perfume*, he realized. "Good Lord," he whispered.

The stairs that David descended were metal and they clanged dully with each footfall.

Below, the tall rectangle of light that was the exit to the street grew no larger as he descended, and he wished desperately that he could see the stairs he was on, that he could see his own feet on them, that he could see himself *actually descending*, actually going down to the first floor.

He wept. He felt trapped here, in this building, in this place.

He said as he wept, "My name is David Case, my name is David Case," and as he said it, as he wept, as he descended the metal stairs—*clang, clang, clang*—the meaning and importance of the words grew and faded, grew and faded, like a heart pumping, a heart losing air.

Christian Grieg lay beside the body that lay halfway in the doorway of the green cottage. He was on his back. He said, with tight excitement, his unfocused gaze on the top of the doorway above him, "I destroyed a fish that the seagulls wanted, David."

An almost imperceptible groan escaped the body beside him.

"I brought my foot down, *sploosh!*" Christian said, and his arms tightened with the memory, "onto that fish and it was no more!" He smiled.

He turned his head so he was looking at the closed eyes of the body in the doorway, whose head had turned toward him. "Listen to me, my friend." He rolled toward David, reached, slapped David's cheek softly. "Listen to me. Open your eyes." He slapped David harder, lifted one of Da-

vid's eyelids; the pupil had ascended,. he saw only
white. "Disgusting," he said.

He rolled to his back again, focused on the top
of the doorway above him. "This is very pleasant,
isn't it?" He grinned. "Two pals having a chat."

A car passed by swiftly on Sylvan Beach Road.

The body beside Christian groaned once more.
Louder. But not loud enough that anyone farther
away than Christian was now could have heard it.

Christian said, still grinning, gaze still on the
doorway above him, "That was a purely rhetorical
comment, I assume."

He rolled his head to the side so he was looking
again at David's closed eyes. There was movement
in them. David's eyes were moving behind his
closed eyelids. Christian lifted one of the lids. He
saw David's light blue iris and dilated black pupil
staring back. A quick, "Ah!" of surprise escaped
him and he let David's eyelid go. His grin vanished. Returned.

He said, gaze still on David's face, "That was a
neat trick, my friend. You scared the piss out of
me."

He put his hand on David's chest. He thought
that there was movement. He wasn't sure. It was
very subtle. It could have been his own hand trembling with excitement.

He lifted David's eyelid again. He saw the light
blue pupil, the dilated black iris staring back. The
iris began to contract as daylight found it.

Christian said, "Are you in there, my friend?"
He paused, continued, "Or is this just some ran-
domness of your bioelectronics—I want to know!"
The fierceness of his last comment surprised him.
Some untapped and unknown reserve of anger?
he wondered.

What was the exact breadth and width of his
power and anger?

He was intrigued.

Clearly, the smashing of the fish was only a minute part of his capabilities.

Look at the wild creatures. The natural creatures that existed on the earth. Look at their power, their anger!

Anne, the woman with the crown of black hair, the fish—what he had done to them was nothing compared with his true power.

He was still staring into David's eye. David's eye was still staring back. Christian said tightly, "You see me here, don't you? I know that you do." He slapped his open hand onto David's chest again and stopped breathing a moment.

Yes. There was movement.

He jumped to his feet, leaned over, grabbed David with both hands by the neck, yanked his body up toward him. "Damn you! Damn you!"

He couldn't suck the air from David anymore. That time had passed.

He had to do something else.

Something more overt.

It was no longer a doorway that David was seeing below, down the black stairway, and his feet no longer *clanged* on the metal stairs. He was seeing something else.

The metal stairs were gone.

The building was gone.

He was seeing light ahead, below, beyond him.

He was seeing an opening.

Movement.

"David Case!" he whispered. "David Case." The words came out and he heard them, but he heard them as if they were at a great distance, and were being shouted to him by someone else.

He had no idea what the words meant.

"Damn you!" he heard.

He saw a face in the opening, in the light. It was a face that was alive with anger, it was surrounded by darkness, and it was shouting. "Damn you!" it shouted, "Damn you!" as he—David—slid toward the opening, as the opening widened and drew him closer, like a mouth taking in food, "Damn you! Damn you!" the face in the opening shouted, "Damn you!" the face shouted, "I brought my foot down *sploosh!*" the face shouted, "onto that fish and it was no more!"

Christian lifted David's body, held it in his arms. David's head fell backwards. His eyes opened halfway.

Christian left the cottage, and headed toward the lake.

David saw blue sky, now. He saw the tips of pine trees. A gull soaring.

EIGHT

"**U**hdarcknass," wrote the chunky man in the below-ground-level apartment, "like knowuthar chasez hymn awl over thuh plas—and he looks bahk and ittz ganeingon hymn fasst, he's knott wonteeng 2b quick enuf oar he wants it to catch hymn, this theeng frum insid hymn. it chaases lika dawg awoolf, a murdereeng theeng and it wonts2 overwelm hymn, eat hymn, mak hymn itself, butt hee is of a bettr mynd and duz not want 2 go 4evr in2 darcknass"

The man fishing from his small outboard motorboat at the center of Oneida Lake was the only person on the lake this windy day, and he was seriously considering going back to land because it looked like a storm was brewing.

He scanned the sky to the north, then to the west and east, then to the south. Solid overcast. God, when had those clouds come in?

Movement on land a quarter mile south caught his eye. He looked. His distance vision was very good but he could not be sure that he was seeing correctly. Was someone being carried toward the lake? Clearly, it was only a prank.

He glanced at the sky again.

Yes, a storm was coming.

He stowed his fishing gear quickly and started the outboard.

Soon, he was headed north, toward home.

After a few moments, he looked back, toward shore.

In the house that once belonged to Anne Case, Dorian fumbles for the light switch so he can go upstairs to the bathroom. He's feeling a little nervous because he can't find the light switch—he's never been to the house before—and though he isn't usually afraid of the darkness, here, on the stairs above him, it makes him nervous because his friends are still gathered in a circle and are waiting for him so they can continue with their séance.

"Where's the light switch?" he calls.

"At the top of the stairs," Maude calls back from the opposite end of the big living room.

"At the top of the stairs?" He's incredulous. Why would anyone put a light switch only at the top of the stairs? "You mean there isn't one down here?"

"That's what I mean."

"Oh."

"Do you want us to turn on one of these lights?"

"No," he answers at once. "It's all right."

He starts up the stairs.

He stops after a moment and peers hard into the darkness.

He believes that he sees something above him, on the landing. Something tall and stocky and mannish. Something with a large, oddly shaped head.

And he hears weeping, too, but very distantly, as if from behind the closed door of a huge room.

He looks back, toward Maude and the rest of the group. When he looks back, he sees nothing. But he can still hear weeping.

He goes upstairs.

A dog ran loose on the rocky beach where Christian carried David. The dog was small, white, skittish. Every few moments, she glanced over her shoulder. She was looking for two things—her owners, and other dogs that roamed freely around Sylvan Beach, one of which had already attacked her and had left her bleeding from her right flank.

Christian saw the dog heading his way and stopped walking. He said, "Hello, doggie," but the dog, busy glancing over her shoulder, didn't notice him at first.

In the opening, in the light surrounded by darkness, David saw the lake, the beach. A white dog.

"Hello, doggie," he heard.

"Hello, doggie!" Christian repeated, angry that the dog hadn't responded. He—Christian—was a wholly natural and spontaneous creature talking to another wholly natural and spontaneous creature, and he deserved a response.

The dog noticed him at last. She stopped walking abruptly and stared wide-eyed up at him, from ten feet away.

"Well, *say* something!" Christian insisted. "I can't stand here all day!" David was getting heavy. The rocks were slippery. The wind was cold.

The dog continued to look at him. She didn't know where to go. The unspoken message she was getting from this man was a message of anger, and the dog had dealt with much human anger in her life. But the lake was in one direction, and the other dog was behind her somewhere, and the road—cars—in the direction that remained, so the dog was at a real loss as to what to do. So, she did nothing. She froze.

Christian advanced slowly on her. "Don't just *look* at me, dog. I'm *talking* to you. I am a *natural creature*, just as you are, and I am talking to you. I *expect* a coherent reply, dammit!"

Still the dog did not move. She sensed that, at any moment, the human would lash out at her. Humans had done that before. Often. She expected it. But still there was the lake in that direction, and the big, dark dog behind her, and the road over there—

"You will *speak* when you're spoken to!" Christian bellowed, and he kicked out at the dog.

The rocks were slippery.

His foot lost purchase.

". . . he's knott wonteeng 2b quik enuf oar he wants it to catch hymn, this theeng frum insid hymn. it chaases lika dawg awoolf, a murdereeng theeng and it wonts2 overwelm hymn, eat hymn, mak hymn itself, butt hee is of a bettr mynd and duz not want 2 go 4evr in2 darcknass and so hee runz and runz awl the time—god hee haz 2 oar it will kach up with hymn . . ."

Christian started to go back. His arms flailed desperately. Futilely. He fell.

David fell with him.

Christian hit the rocky beach. First his lower

back hit, which did no damage, then his left elbow, at the funny bone, which sent a flurry of pain up his arm; then his upper back, onto flat rocks, then the back of his head. He felt that. He lay for the briefest moment—one beat of a humming-bird's wings—with his head supported at an awkward angle by a rock and his gaze wide and disbelieving.

Then David fell on top of him, across his chest, facedown.

There was a loud, moist crack as Christian's neck broke.

The little white dog scurried off, feet scrabbling for a hold on the slippery rocks.

David saw light all around.

He felt wind on his face and back.

He smelled lake air. Fish. He heard the sound of something scurrying off.

What in the hell was he doing out here?

Somebody was beneath him.

"My God!" he whispered.

He tried his arms. They would not begin to lift him.

He tried to see who it was beneath him, tried to turn his head. It was no use. He saw only a hand, palm up, fingers curled slightly, on the rocks near his face. The hand was very close. Out of focus.

It was daylight in the room and nothing moved, except the dust. It covered everything. It moved as if from the force of wind, though there was no wind. It rose and scattered and collected itself, it wafted into the space of the room, settled, and collected.

The dust was dark. Like the earth.

It was made of earth.

* * *

"Are you all right?" David heard from a distance. He wanted to look up, to see who was calling. But he couldn't.

"Are you *all right*?" the voice repeated.

"No!" David managed, his voice barely more than a whisper. "Help me!" But the wind covered the sound of his voice. Even he did not hear it.

In the room the days came and went like leaves turning over in a wind. Time was not measured well by them; the days measured only the passing of events—snow fell and covered the house to a depth of several inches, then was gone; a breeze passed through the house, pushed the dust about, and when it dissipated, the dust collected itself again.

The dust was sturdy and brown. It sat up a little as it collected itself, then it lay down again.

In the cellar, the things that existed there slithered up the stairs, pushing the darkness ahead of them as they moved, out the doors, over the windowsills.

They found the fields of clover empty.

They went into the cities; they pushed the darkness ahead of them as they moved.

And they found the cities empty.

They went back to their cellar.

They waited.

"Are you all right?" asked the face above David. It was a round face, gentle, old, and caring. The gray eyes were full of sympathy, the weathered cheeks raw and red from the cold wind.

"No," David managed. "I'm hurt."

"Yes," said the face, "I can see that. Let me help you." David felt himself being lifted by strong arms. "I'm afraid your friend is very badly hurt."

"Yes," David said.
"Perhaps worse."
David said nothing.

In the dark room, the dust collected itself, and stood. It looked about, and was frightened.

The dust felt no tug of gravity. It felt a tug from above. This was, at once, strange and comforting.

Eventually, the dust collected itself sufficiently that it scratched at an itch that had always bothered it. Then it stood and, without real purpose, moved about in the room. At last, it went back to where it had arisen.

It lay down.
It wept.
It laughed.
It remembered.
This is what it remembered:

Beverly looked at Stephen, and she saw a monster, something with a huge, misshapen head and bulbous eyes and a long, greedy tongue. She loved what she saw. *This* was her Stephen, and she knew that he was seeing her the same way, for the first time, and that he loved what he was seeing, too. Loved every repulsive, slavering, greedy, *human* part of her.

Two monsters fucking. It was *real*, it was *good*, it would *last*.

The dust smiled as it remembered the words. The words told it much.

The dust could create itself from them.

"If you'll be all right for a moment—"
"Please, don't leave," David pleaded.

"I've got to see to your friend," the round-faced man explained.

David closed his eyes in assent.

"I won't be long, I promise. Does your phone work?"

"Phone?"

"I've got to call someone to help you."

"Oh. Yes. It works." David was beginning to feel a little stronger. The man had laid him on the couch. He found that he was strong enough to sit up a little, and prop himself up with his arm, though only for a moment. Then he plopped back down again. "The phone's in the kitchen."

The man nodded. "Let me go get your friend, first."

"Yes," David said. "I'll be all right."

At the house, the dust settled, formed, dissipated, collected again, rose, went to the doorway, stood there, its huge misshapen head and bulbous eyes—its real self, the self it had always so wanted to be—and mannish body turned toward fields not far off.

In the fields surrounding the house, people were picking fruit that grew on plants which hung close to the ground. This fruit was sweet, pungent, and red, like strawberries, and one of the people gathering the fruit straightened in the white light, held a piece of the fruit between his fingers and smiled. "We could have whipped cream with this," he said.

There were people around him, but they made no acknowledgment of him. And the man, having already forgotten what he had said, popped the fruit into his mouth, enjoyed the squish of it under his tongue, and continued picking.

The dust left the house.
Eventually, it found its way to a road.
Behind him, the darkness came.

Karen Duffy, fixing dinner for herself, felt very
unclean.

She had let Christian make love to her not too
long ago. She had *enjoyed* it, had enjoyed his
kisses, had hungered after him, had wanted his
hands on her.

Now, knowing what he was—

She stopped her thoughts there. What could she
prove? What could anyone prove? His letters and
Anne's writings amounted to nothing more than
scraps of paper, really.

It was no consolation. She *knew* what he had
done, even if she had no real proof. What proof
did she need? She wasn't about to point the finger
at him.

Perhaps, even if she had proof, she wouldn't do
anything. He had himself to live with, after all.
Perhaps that was punishment enough.

No, she corrected herself almost furiously. If
she had proof, he would be behind bars at that
very moment.

She put her dinner preparations in the cup-
board. Suddenly, she didn't feel like eating. She
wondered if she would ever feel like eating again.

"How is he?" David managed.

"Your friend?" asked the round-faced man. He
had lain Christian's body on the deck, not wanting
to upset David. "I'm not sure." He gestured toward the back of the living room. "Kitchen's that
way?"

David nodded.

* * *

The dust that had become a man sensed the darkness behind it on the road.

The man turned, faced the darkness, and smiled.

He welcomed the darkness.

He embraced it.

It had always been his friend.

NINE

It is ten years later and, in the house where Anne Case once lived, Dorian, who had excused himself to use the bathroom, rejoins the circle and says to Maude, "I didn't mean to wake anyone up. I'm sorry."

Maude gives him a questioning look. "I don't understand."

"Apparently I woke one of your children. I heard him crying. I'm sorry." He takes the hand of the woman beside him. He's ready to continue with the séance.

"You heard crying?" Maude asks.

Dorian nods. "Yes. When I was going upstairs. It sounded like it was on the stairs with me, at first, and that got me going, I'll tell you." He grins, embarrassed. "I even convinced myself that I saw something up there. On the landing." Another embarrassed grin. "Then I realized that the crying was coming from one of the rooms up there, one of the bedrooms, it was so distant—"

"We don't have any children," Maude cuts in.

"But I heard crying," Dorian insists. "Like someone was having a nightmare. Exactly like someone was having a nightmare." He pauses. The others look dubiously at him. He continues, "You know, the kind of nightmare that's not so horrific that it makes you scream, or wake up. The kind that's . . . claustrophobic, I guess." Again he pauses. Again, no one says anything. "The kind that makes you sweat," he continues. "Like whoever was crying was . . . trapped." He smiles nervously. "Like he was locked up somewhere—" *In the dark, forever!* he thinks.

The others look dumbly at him.

He says, "Trapped alone in the dark. Forever."

The others gathered in the house say nothing. There's some nervous fidgeting.

Dorian looks silently at them.

He looks toward the stairs.

He looks at the group again.

"Thanks anyway," he says to them at last. "But I don't think that I want to be here with you."

He stands and quickly leaves the house.

The woman in the small, elegantly furnished room wrote, "Dyeeng dyeeng draseena leaf." She stopped. She pursed her lips. *Draseena?* she wondered. What a very pleasant sounding word.

She continued writing.

She wrote voluminously.

She wrote of the *draseena*, of *air*, of *open spasis*, of *Brien* and *Kristienne* and *Dayveed*.

Her words came out effortlessly onto the paper. She put them into short, pleasant lines, and the pleasant lines into shapes on the paper; these shapes made her smile.

Sometimes, as she wrote, she read to the young man with her in the room, and he nodded and smiled afterward and told her that he was comfortable having her read to him.

Once, she glanced at the walls of the little room and a shiver ran through her.

That's when she wrote, "The man with thuh nife iz in a bocks!" She wrote it again and again; "The man with thuh nife iz in a bocks! The man with thuh nife iz in a bocks! The man with thuh nife iz in a bocks!" At last, the young man with her, sensing her discomfort, went to her and put his pale hands on her shoulders, leaned over and whispered, "Let's go out, now."

"To where?" she asked.

"Anywhere. These walls are so . . . confining."

She looked at him for a long while without speaking. Then she rose and, arm in arm, they went out into the light.